Strange Capers

Henry James Garon

DEDICATION

For my mother, who read stories to us as we sat in her lap
in the big chair in the living room.

CONTENTS

ACKNOWLEDGMENTS

My dad was a Hollywood publicist, and a big fan of Rod Serling. When my dad was still in school, he worked with Rod Serling at one of the networks, and he prevailed upon Mr. Serling to speak at his graduation. I watched re-runs of *The Twilight Zone* many times growing up, and I always wanted to write those types of stories. I guess I inherited my love of Rod Serling from my dad. So thanks to Rod Serling and my dad.

Thanks to my mother for reading stories to me when I was a toddler. Thanks also to my mother and my brother Johnny for putting up with me. Thanks to all my family for all of the laughs and all of the fights over nothing.

Thanks to all the many people who write blogs giving advice on how to self-publish, how to fix your computer, and how to cool off a beer really fast.

And thanks to God, who invented me out of whole cloth.

1 STRANGE CAPERS

We that are true lovers run into strange capers. But as all is mortal in nature, so is all nature in love mortal in folly.

Joe hid under his blanket with his back to the dresser. He closed his eyes tightly and spoke quietly under his breath:

"It isn't there. It didn't happen. I didn't do anything. It's yesterday again, and I haven't gone to the store yet."

Joe turned back to the dresser, lifted his blanket, and stared at the dresser's top drawer. He arose and walked over to the brightly stained wooden dresser. He opened the top drawer slowly, closing it quickly as soon as he saw the dark green bag from the jeweler's shop. Joe ran back to his bed and covered himself with his blanket again. How could everything have gone so wrong?

Just the day before Joe had first seen the Christmas advertisement from the jeweler's, and it seemed like the perfect gift. For Lisa.

Joe had never even thought of girls before Lisa. She was new to the school, and she sat in front of Joe. On the first day of sixth grade, Lisa sat in front of Joe, and all of this blondish-light-brown hair spilled over the back of her chair, and onto the front of his desk.

Lisa's hair was kind of wild, and it had little ringlets that went all over the place. Lisa didn't seem overly preoccupied with her hair, but she would often wear a ribbon or a hair clip.

And Joe felt strange about Lisa's hair. It smelled of flowers. Almost every day some of her hair was on the front of his desk, and Joe didn't mind at all. He wanted to touch Lisa's hair, but he didn't, because he didn't her to think he was creepy. Joe wondered if her hair was soft or hard. He imagined that Lisa's hair was soft because Lisa was so nice. If she ever had to pass something back to Joe, she always smiled sweetly. Joe would always smile back at her. Joe had never thought about smiling at girls before, and now he thought about smiling at Lisa a lot.

And the months passed. Soon it was Christmas break, and Joe had three weeks off before returning to school in the new year. Joe still thought of Lisa, but he wouldn't see her for a few weeks. And then the color circular arrived in the mail. The local jeweler had a sale on gold chains: "This Christmas, why not buy a beautiful 18k gold chain for that special someone?"

Joe looked at the chain on the circular and it reminded him of Lisa's hair. Golden. 'Lisa had golden hair', he thought. There was a warm feeling he had when he thought of Lisa and he liked it. Joe examined the circular closely. "That special someone." Joe had thought of putting the chain around Lisa's neck. "It matches your hair," he saw himself saying to Lisa in his mind's eye. He saw her giving him one of her little smiles, and the warm feeling came over him again.

So that was the start of the idea. Joe had money saved up from mowing lawns, and his mother went shopping for gifts at the mall that evening. She let him slip away to buy his own things. Joe bought a video game and then, making sure he wasn't followed, Joe trotted straight over to the jewelers.

The jewelry store was doing a brisk business. There were many people lined up to make purchases at the counter, and all the salespeople were busy helping customers. Joe looked at the display of chains that were in the advertisement, locked up in a display case. There were stacks of thin, rectangular white boxes with glossy lids.

"Can I help you?"

Joe looked up at the tall sales lady who was smiling at him. She had blond hair too, but it wasn't as nice as Lisa's, Joe thought.

"Yes, I would like one of the chains, please."

The sales lady smiled. "We've been selling a lot of these," she said.

She unlocked the case and took a box from the top of the stack. The saleslady's hands had long fingers that expertly opened the lid and displayed the golden chain inside. The thin gold chain was sitting on top of a bed of cotton, with a small tag assuring the buyer that it was 18 carat, gold-plated over sterling.

"Perfect," Joe said.

The sales lady put the box into a sales bag and put the bag on the counter. She smiled at Joe and entered the item into the register.

"Will that be all?" she asked.

Joe reached out for the bag. "Uhm…". He hadn't considered whether there would be anything else. His vision had always been one of him putting a chain around Lisa's neck and telling her that it matched her hair. "I don't know," Joe said.

"Perhaps a pendant to go on the chain?" the saleslady offered.

She led Joe over to the display case where there was a vast array of little golden slippers, jeweled hearts, small golden constellations, and precious stones. "Do you see anything that you like? Is this for your mother? Is there something that your mother likes? For example, if she likes music, you could get a musical note pendant."

Joe didn't want to tell the lady that he was buying the pendant for a girl in his class. "I don't know," he said.

"Perhaps a stone," the saleslady said. She pointed to another section where there were pendants of precious stones, and Joe's eyes fastened on a pendant that was the same color as Lisa's eyes.

"That one's nice," Joe said, pointing.

The saleslady opened the display case and pulled the stone down from the display. "That's a sapphire," she said. "That's very nice. That will look just lovely on that chain. Would you like this as well?"

Joe smiled. "Yes. That's perfect."

The saleslady fitted the pendant into a small jewelry case and handed it to Joe. "There you go. Someone at the counter will ring you up."

Joe was thinking about how much Lisa would like the chain and the pendant that matched her eyes. He hadn't quite figured out how he was going to give it to her yet. The lady behind the counter rang up the purchase, and put the pendant into the dark green bag that held the chain.

The total was a lot less than Joe had expected to pay. Joe suspected that the lady had not charged him for one of the items, but he didn't say anything.

Joe placed the jeweler's bag on the bottom of the bag with the video game, and started over to the coffee

shop where he was to meet his mother.   He looked at
the receipt. The lady at the counter had charged him for
the pendant but had forgotten the chain. Joe checked the
bag again, and the chain was there.

'She only had to ring up two things and she missed
one of them?'

Joe looked back at the store. There was a line of
people waiting to purchase.

'I shouldn't have to wait in line again. Plus, I'm
going to be late to meet Mom,' he thought.

Joe turned to go to the coffee shop. He took a
couple of steps. 'I didn't pay for the chain. That's
stealing,' he thought. Joe made a few steps back towards
the jewelry store.

Joe stopped. 'But I paid what the lady asked me
for. It's not my fault she can't do her stupid job."

Joe started walking towards that coffee shop again.
If people were watching from the upper level of the
shopping mall, they could have seen Joe halt several
times, check his bag, glance in the direction of the jewelry
store, and then set off back towards that coffee shop.

Joe's mother asked him what was wrong, and Joe
said that he just felt tired. He sat there with his mother
and sipped at his iced mocha, saying nothing. Joe's
conscience condemned him, but he dared not to say a
word to his mother because he did not want her to think
he was a thief. His father came home from work that
night and asked Joe what was wrong.

"Nothing," Joe said.

Joe's parents shrugged their shoulders and
wondered what had happened to make their normally
happy and carefree boy so sullen.

The next day, Joe was lying in bed with his back to

the dresser, and his mother called out from downstairs.

"Joe, are you coming down to breakfast?"

Joe's little brother and sister were already in their places at the table, eating sausages and giggling. Joe's father was looking at the morning paper. Joes' mother put a plate of waffles and sausages before him. Joe stared down at his plate.

"They caught the guys who held up the drugstore in Wakefield," his father said.

"That was fast," Joe's mother said.

Joe put his head in his hands.

"Are you alright, Joey?" his mother asked.

"I'm just tired," Joe said.

"Apparently one of the robbers tried to pawn off some of the watches they stole. They always make a mistake, these guys," his father said.

Joe stared at his waffles. His brother and sister laughed about something, and happily chewed their waffles.

Later, Joe sat up in his room and looked at the dresser. The answer came to him suddenly. "I could just take the chain back to the store," he thought. "I'll just say that the lady didn't ring up the chain, and I didn't notice until I got home."

Joe opened up the drawer, took the bag out, and looked at the receipt. Joe put the pendant onto the chain and put them both into one box. He dressed warmly in his heavy jacket and put the jewelry box into his jacket pocket.

The bus only took ten minutes to get to the mall, and Joe soon found himself in the jewelry store again. He had intended to walk straight to the counter, but a disturbance began just as he entered the store. It seems that a young man, a little older than Joe, had been caught stealing. The manager, a man of about 40 was leaning over the erstwhile jewelry thief. He spoke with a slight Italian accent.

"I should call the cops, you know?" the manager said. "Why do you steal from me?"

The manager was not a big man, but his voice sounded scary to Joe.

"You gonna give me your momma's phone number and she's going to have to come and get you. You gonna have to tell your momma what you did. You gonna tell her that you stole."

The boy was crying, but he knew it was better to have to confess to his mother than to be arrested by the police.

The manager held the boy by the shoulder and escorted him back behind the counter, and into a little office.

"Can I help you?" A sales lady had appeared out of nowhere.

Joe reached into his pocket for the receipt. It wasn't there! He checked his other pocket. 'What happened to the receipt?'

"Uhm, just a second," Joe said.

Joe's face grew hot. He was suddenly very conscious that he had a box of jewelry in his pocket, and that he hadn't paid for half of it. Joe started to have a vision of being cornered by the manager, and accused of being a thief.

Joe was starting to sweat. He opened his jacket. 'What if the box fell out of his jacket and onto the floor?'

Joe checked all of his pockets, and he could not find the receipt.

"I think I forgot something," Joe said. "I'll come

back."

Joe turned and walked out of the store. He wanted to run out as fast as he could, but he was afraid he would look suspicious.

He walked down to the coffee shop and ordered an iced chocolate. 'How can I do this without looking like I stole it? It's not like I'm trying to take anything. I just want to give them some money.'

Joe pondered over his problem while watching the line of customers in the coffee shop. A little old lady dropped something, and the boy behind her picked it up. The boy tapped the lady on the shoulder and handed it to her. It was money! The lady thanked the boy and smiled at him. And the idea came to Joe: he would go back into the jewelry store and "find" a fifty-dollar bill on the floor. The chain only came to $38 with tax, but Joe could hardly "find" a twenty, a ten, a five, and three ones. No, he would "find" a $50 bill and give it to the store manager, and the manager would smile at him just like the little old lady had done.

Joe had gone to the bank and gotten a $50 bill. The bill was brand new, and Joe thought that looked suspicious, so he crumpled it up a few times on the way to the jewelry store. He folded the bill over and palmed it under his thumb, and walked behind one of the display cases. Checking to see that he was not noticed, Joe reached down onto the carpet and "found" the $50 bill.

The manager was behind the counter looking at a stack of invoices. Joe held the $50 bill before him.

"I found this on the floor," Joe lied.

The manager did not look up from his work. "It's not mine," he said.

"But I found it in your store," Joe said, handing the

bill over the counter.

The manager reached up and stopped Joe's hand, and looked down at him. "That's not mine, kid," the manager said.

"Maybe somebody dropped it in the store," Joe said.

"I know that legally the money belongs to me," the manager said. "But I don't operate that way. If someone wants to buy something, they come into my store, I sell them something and they give me the money. But if I go around laying claim to all the money found in my store, then I'm going to be a greedy guy. And if I'm a greedy guy, then I'll turn into a cheat. And I'm not gonna be no cheat."

Joe stood at the counter, wondering what to do.

The manager looked up and smiled kindly. "Look: I know you're an honest kid. You found that money, and as far as I'm concerned, it belongs to you now. If you want to buy something, then you can give it to me. Otherwise, you just hang on to it, okay?"

The manager went to help a customer, and Joe walked out of the jewelry store shaking his head.

Joe's father returned home on Christmas Eve. The two youngest children had been drawing Christmas cards, and they ran to meet him at the door. Joe's father approved of their fine work, and they returned to their work table to make more.

Joe's father smiled. The house looked very festive: a Christmas tree stood in the far corner of the living room, trimmed in blinking colored lights and tinsel, and five stockings hung from the chimney. He smelled cookies baking in the kitchen, and Joe's mother was putting the top crust on an apple pie.

He gave his wife a kiss. "That smells great, Hon," he said.

Joe's father noticed that his wife was frowning. "What's wrong? Did the kids break something?"

"It's Joey. He's been just sitting in his room all day. He seems depressed. I'm worried. He's never been like this before."

"Well, he's getting into puberty now," Joe's father said. "It's probably a crush. I'll go talk to him."

Joe was in his bed, with his head under the covers and his back to the dresser. Joe's father sat on the edge of the bed.

"What's up, Champ?" he said.

Joe looked out from under the covers. "Hi Dad," Joe said.

"It's Christmas tomorrow," Joe's dad said. "Is that why you're depressed?"

Joe sighed and turned to the wall. A tear leaked down the side of his face.

"Look, Joey. You've been moping around here for the last few days. I know you're upset about something, but I can't help you if you won't tell me what it is."

Joe turned back and looked at his dad. He didn't want to tell his dad that he stole, but he didn't have any other options. Joe's eyes welled up with tears. "You're not going to like me if I tell you," he said.

Joe's dad bent down and gave his son a very strong hug, and kissed him firmly on the forehead. "Who said I like you now?" his father said.

Joe laughed. "Okay, well there's this girl…"

And Joe told his dad all about Lisa, and the chain, and the jewelry store. Joe's dad listened patiently and nodded. When Joe was finished he looked up his dad expectantly.

"I see," his father said. "Well, that's quite an interesting predicament. I can help you fix this all up, but it's going to be a little tough for you."

Joe thought about it. "I'll do anything," he said. "I can't stand feeling sad and guilty all the time. I want to go back to the way I was before."

"It can be that way, but you have to trust your old man and do everything I say. Can you do that?"

Joe nodded.

"Okay, this is what you need to do…"

The jewelry store was closing in a half hour. There were some last-minute shoppers, but the store was fairly quiet. The manager was thinking about where he would take his family for dinner when he saw that kid stride in carrying a bag from the store.

"Hey, kid. What can I help you with?" The manager noticed that the kid had tear streaks on his face.

Joe put the bag on the counter. "I want to return this necklace," he said.

"Of course," the manager said. "You want a refund?"

"No," Joe said. "I didn't pay for it." Joe took the fifty-dollar bill out of his pocket and put it on the counter.

The manager opened up the jewelry box and saw that there was a pendant on the chain. "I don't get it," he said.

"I paid for the pendant, but the lady didn't ring up the chain, and I let her do it. So I walked out without paying for it."

"Okay, no problem," the manager said. He rang up the price for the chain and handed Joe the change. Joe put the change in his pocket and turned to go.

"Hey, kid, don't you want the chain? You paid for it."

Joe turned around. "My dad and I agreed that when I walked out of here without paying for the chain, that was stealing. Stealing is what greedy people do. I don't want to be a greedy person, and I don't want to be a thief. You understand that, don't you sir?"

"Hey, kid, I can't take your money for nothing," the manager said.

"Look, mister. I know you're an honest guy. But I promised my dad that I would leave this here, and I'm going to do exactly what he told me to do. Merry Christmas."

Joe turned and walked quickly out of the store before anyone could stop him.

He could hear the manager behind him. "What is he doing? I can't take this. You gotta talk to him..."

Before he had even left the store Joe felt his heart returning to normal. A great weight had been lifted from his shoulders. His dad was right! It worked. Joe looked around the mall and felt joyful that it would soon be Christmas.

Joe's parents sat in the car waiting for their son. The younger ones were asleep in their car seats.

"I can understand why he had to make a full confession," Joe's mother said. "But why did he have to return everything after paying for it?"

Joe's father nodded. "I know it seems harsh, but there's an ulterior motive here. If I make the punishment really bad, then he won't feel guilty because he was punished. He already suffered from guilt, so making him lose a lot of money ought to compensate for that. But the other part is giving a chain to a girl at that age. He doesn't even hardly know her. How's he going to give a girl a chain with a pendant? That's a little awkward, don't you think?"

"Yeah, I guess," Joe's mother said.

"This way, Joe will have to get to know her in a normal way first. If they become good friends, then he can get her a ribbon or something. He can work his way up to buying her some jewelry."

"That makes sense," Joe's mother said. She snuggled her head up to her husband's arm, and they both smiled at nothing in particular.

Joe was nearly out of the building when he heard a girl's voice behind him. "Joe! Wait!"

Joe turned around. It was Lisa! She was wearing a long skirt, and her hair fell loosely on a button-up white sweater that she wore open. Lisa had a little Santa cap on her head.

Joe felt a warm feeling come over him, and he smiled awkwardly. "What are you doing here?"

Lisa held up the jewelry bag. "My dad owns the jewelry store," she said. "He said that you left this at the counter, and he told me that I had to make sure you took it."

Joe's heart sunk. He knew he couldn't take the chain back. He just got back to normal.

"Look, Lisa," he began.

She looked at him, not understanding. Joe didn't want to argue with her.

Joe took the bag from her. "I'll tell you what I'm going to do. Tell your dad that I'll compromise: I'll take it back, but it's mine to give. So I'm going to give it to you."

"Okay," Lisa said.

Joe opened the box and took the chain out. "Turn around," he said to Lisa.

Lisa turned around without hesitating. Joe swept her hair onto her right shoulder, and expertly fit the chain around her neck, fastening the clasp like a pro. Joe noticed that Lisa's hair was, in fact, very soft and smelled of herbs.

"There," Joe said. "Let me see you."

Lisa turned around to face Joe. She had a broad smile, but she looked down sheepishly.

"It goes with your hair. You really do have golden hair," he said.

Lisa looked up. "Thank you," she said.

The stone nearly perfectly matched her eyes. "You look like a million bucks," Joe said. "Tell your dad we're even, okay?"

"Okay," Lisa said.

The two of them smiled at each other for a moment. Joe said, "My mom and dad are waiting for me in the car. I'll see you after the break, okay?"

"Okay."

"Merry Christmas, Lisa!"

"Merry Christmas, Joe!" Lisa waved to Joe as he left the mall.

Lisa walked back to her father's store and touched the little blue stone. She already had one of the chains from her father's store. She owned several chains, but this one was her favorite. She looked at the large Christmas tree in the mall entrance and smiled at nothing in particular.

The End

2 SHORT SHRIFT

Ratcliffe: Come, come, dispatch: the Duke would be at dinner;
Make a short shrift: he longs to see your head.

Hastings: O momentary grace of mortal men,
Which we more hunt for than the grace of God!

Goody Fleure relaxed when he saw the man in the
blue suit. Goody had seen the man several times before,
and he considered the man to be a good omen.

Only a year before, in 1937, he had been
"discovered" playing at a roadside restaurant in Durham,
NY. The man in the blue suit had been there that night.
At least, Goody firmly believed that he had seen the man
that night.

After that, Goody had signed with an agent, who
arranged a booking tour and a recording contract.
Goody's mother thought that it was all too much for a
young man his age. After all, he had only finished high
school a few years before. But Goody had always wanted
to be a jazz musician, and he had worked tirelessly for the
last ten years to make this come about. He had listened

regularly to the live radio broadcast from the Cotton Club, playing along with Duke Ellington, imagining the time he would be headlining at jazz clubs.

The recording sessions were over in just a couple of days. Goody had been very impressed with the band: a bassist, drummer, and a saxophonist that his agent had put together. The man in the blue suit had been there. Goody was almost positive that he had seen the man in the recording studio.

And now Goody's name and picture were outside the Hideaway Restaurant, in the hills north of the San Fernando Valley. Two giant searchlights lit up the night sky behind the restaurant, and people were paying to see him!

The first set had gone well. The others had gone into the parking lot for a smoke, and Goody decided to soak up the limelight at a table near the stage. That was when he saw the man in the blue suit.

"Do you mind if I join you?"

Goody motioned for the man to sit down. He had never spoken to the man in the blue suit before: it was a dark blue suit that looked custom made, and he wore a red silk tie. He also wore a very fancy wristwatch. To Goody, who came from a small town, the man in blue appeared to be very wealthy. The man was smaller than Goody, and he wore his black hair neatly oiled.

"My name's Specter," the man said. He shook Goody's hand lightly and asked for the waiter to bring champagne.

Goody wondered if he should be drinking before the next set.

'A glass or two wouldn't hurt,' he thought to

himself, although he knew that his mother wouldn't approve of his drinking alcohol in a nightclub. This was the very sort of situation that his mother had warned against when Goody had been offered the tour.

Mr. Specter smiled broadly as he poured the champagne. "You have a very unique voice," he said. This was similar to what the agent had said. Goody thanked the man and drank deeply from the champagne, wondering what Specter had come to speak to him about.

"I heard the recordings you cut last month. I think you're going to have a few hit songs on your hands," Specter said.

"But how...," Goody started. "I thought that the record hadn't been released yet."

"It hasn't. None of your recordings have been officially released, but I ... heard them already. I'm a great fan of yours," Specter smiled.

Goody imagined that Mr. Specter was a very successful man in the record industry, and that was how he was able to hear the recordings. He smiled. A record executive was already a big fan of his. Things were looking up. It was fate. Goody had always known that he would be a big recording star, and he had worked hard for it. He planned to tour the states for a few years, and then he would travel to France, and play in the Hot Club of Paris. Goody always wanted to meet Django Reinhardt and Stéphane Grappelli.

"You're very young to be out on the road by yourself," Specter said.

The question took Goody by surprise. "Yes," he said. "My mother felt the same way." Goody put his forehead into his hand and rubbed it, thinking back.

Specter refilled Goody's glass, and Goody thought about the argument he had had with his mother just before he left home. He had never fought with his mother before, and the moment always filled him with regret when it was brought to mind. His mother did not trust his agent or any of the people he was working with. She considered it a bad twist of fate that Buddy had been "discovered" at all.

"I'm sure I've seen you before, Mr. Specter."

Specter's eyebrow raised slightly. "I don't recall our meeting."

"The night I met my agent. I'm sure I saw you there."

"I look like a lot of people. Perhaps you were confused," Specter said.

Goody liked the champagne. He was starting to feel light-headed. It felt good. The conversations from the other tables seemed to be louder. Goody was normally reserved, especially when talking to people he didn't know, but his curiosity was overwhelming him now, and he was starting to care less about what the stranger thought of him.

Goody leaned in closer to Specter. "I know it sounds strange, but I know I've seen you before. Many times." Goody finished another glass of champagne. "Even when I was very young. I've noticed that you were present at pivotal times in my life."

"Really?" Specter kept refilling Goody's glass. "That's quite fascinating. It sounds like you were looking forward to meeting me almost as much as I was to meet you."

"You were always wearing the same clothes," Goody said. "When I was very young. My parents bought a piano for me. You were there in the store."

Specter's expression turned to one of disbelief. "Oh, come now, Mr. Fleure. How could I have been?"

"I don't know," Goody said. "It has always been a strange fascination. I would see you at these moments in my life, and I started to associate you with being a good omen."

"Well, that's a very nice compliment." Specter filled both of their glasses and called for more champagne. "But I assure you, Mr. Fleure, I am just an ordinary man. I'm not an angel, or an omen, or anything like that. Perhaps it's just deja vu, or something similar."

"No, it's very real. I know it," Goody said. His face felt flushed, and he wiped his forehead with his hands. The back of his head seemed more sensitive, and he felt as though he could feel all the individual hairs on his head.

Goody looked at Specter. "I've thought about this a lot," he said. "I figured that you could either be a figment of my imagination or …"

"Or an angel?" Specter volunteered.

"Or a time traveler," Goody said.

Specter laughed and then darted a glance over his shoulder. Goody wondered if Specter had come to the restaurant alone.

"A time traveler? Now I wonder if we've had too much champagne," Specter said.

"I'm serious. If you had a time machine, you could travel from the future, after I became famous, back to the day I recorded in the studio."

Specter smiled, and Goody felt his face growing red out of embarrassment. He had never told anyone this before, and hearing himself say such fantastic things made him feel foolish.

Specter put a reassuring hand on Goody's. "Well, I don't own a time machine, but let's entertain your theory." Specter looked at his watch and glanced over his shoulder again. Goody noticed a man in a white hat. The man had been observing them, but he looked away when Goody met his glance.

"If a time machine existed, then there would be the problem of creating a paradox," Specter explained. "For example, a man goes back in time and murders his grandfather before his father was born."

"Well, I can't see why someone would want to murder his grandfather," Goody said.

"Neither can I, but it remains that such a possibility would exist if a time machine existed."

"But that doesn't mean a time machine couldn't exist. Perhaps a paradox would just be self-correcting," Goody said.

"How so?"

Goody took a sip from his champagne and thought for a moment. "Perhaps time would just assign all of that man's actions to other people. Instantaneously. Maybe time would just heal itself: The moment he killed his grandfather, time would be shifted to make up for any paradox. The man's grandmother would have married someone else, and they would have had a child much like the man's father, who would have lived a similar life. Of course, that particular man, and his father would never have existed."

"Very good," Specter said. "You have a talent for abstract thinking. I should have expected as much from a jazz improviser. But we still have the problem of changing history. Your concept of a self-healing time might work, but what if a man were to kill a pivotal figure and change history? Or if a time traveler were to reveal battle plans to an army general? What if the British had been warned that Washington was planning to cross the Delaware? They could have met the colonists on the banks of the Delaware with loaded muskets. History would be changed. No United States. No Constitution. No Civil War. Everything would have been changed."

"I see what you mean," Goody said. "But even still, despite that danger, it doesn't mean that a time machine couldn't exist. It would only mean that a time machine would be a very dangerous affair."

"Yes, but would it make sense to operate such a machine?"

"I don't know. You would have to regulate its use," Goody said.

Specter glanced at his watch and then back behind him again, and moved in closer to Goody. "Okay, let's imagine that a fellow invents a time machine, and he knows what we have figured out. He wants to profit from his invention, but he knows that if he tries to change history in any way, it could cause a great rupture, and he could lose everything. What should he do?"

Goody thought for a moment and drew a deep breath. He was feeling very relaxed from the champagne. "I suppose I would offer a sort of travel service," he said.

"What do you mean?"

"I would sell tickets to people to go back in time, but only as tourists. They could go and live for a time in the past, but they would have to be under strict orders not to change anything. It would be like a vacation. A trip to a distant land," Goody said.

Specter sipped his champagne and nodded thoughtfully. Goody looked down at his shoes, and Specter looked over his shoulder again. Goody looked up and saw that the man in the white hat was still there, but he appeared to be talking to another man at the bar.

"If it were my invention," Specter said, "I would run it on a very exclusive basis. Invitation only. If I had the exclusive right over the time machine, I could charge a pretty penny for a trip to the past."

"How much do you reckon?" Goody asked.

Specter shrugged. "Maybe a million dollars for one trip."

Goody whistled through his teeth. "That would be some business, I guess. But if you think about it, a lot of people are going to want to go to the same time periods. For example, won't a lot of people want to go hear the Gettysburg Address, or watch the Salem witch trials?"

Specter nodded. "I imagine, there would be a limited amount of tickets to those events, and they would probably be priced at a premium. Whereas, if you went someplace where there wasn't much demand, you could probably take several trips for the same price."

"Supply and demand," Goody said. "But how would you protect history? How could you keep an eye on people?"

"I suppose everyone would have to be chaperoned. And there would be rules about what you could bring and what you could take back. As you said, it would have to be fairly regulated."

"And you couldn't change anything," Goody said. "No matter what, you couldn't tell someone that they were sick and to see a doctor. You couldn't tell them not to go on some plane that you knew was going to crash. You had to let it all happen, just the way it had happened in history."

"I guess so," Specter said. "Everyone would have to adopt the attitude of a fatalist. By regulation."

"That would be tough. You would have to let children get hit by cars, or let a theatre full of people die in a fire," Goody said.

"Yep. Even if you knew a dam was going to

collapse at a certain time, you would have to keep that to yourself."

Mr. Specter filled both of their glasses once more. "But that's all hypothetical. We won't that get us down."

Specter and Goody took a drink, and Specter continued: "But I think that a lot of this type of speculation about time machines is just regretting over the past."

"Perhaps you're right," Goody said.

"If you live your life right, you won't have regrets," Specter said.

Goody nodded. "You're probably right." He paused and looked down. "I have some regrets," he said.

"A young man like you? What have you got to regret?"

Goody found himself fighting back a tear. "My mother," he said. "We had a big fight when I left home. I made her cry. My mother worked so hard and gave up everything for me, and that's the way I paid her back. Making my mother cry like that. That's my biggest regret."

"Why don't you call her?" Specter said.

Goody looked at his watch. "It's past twelve where she is. My mother's asleep."

"Call her. I'm sure she'd love to hear from you. Here," Specter fished into his pocket. He gave a short glance over his shoulder, and then pulled out a roll of quarters and put it on the table.

"Are you serious?" Goody asked.

Specter nodded. "I'm completely serious. Your mother would be very happy to hear from you."

Goody took the quarters. "Okay. I will. Thanks, Mr. Specter. I'll be back in a little bit."

"Take your time," Specter said.

Goody hung up the payphone backstage and was drying his eyes with a handkerchief. He had woken his mother up, but she was happy to hear from him. Goody had apologized profusely and told his mother that he loved her. She was crying too. It was a good call.

Although Goody felt greatly relieved, he was still feeling the effects of the champagne. He looked at his watch. The next show was going to start in ten minutes, and Goody wondered how well he was going to play.

The stage lights were still off, and from backstage Goody could see the restaurant clearly, but he couldn't see Specter at the table anymore. He decided to see how the band was doing out in the back. Just then he heard a loud crack like an explosion in a pile of rocks. Goody hurried towards that back door that opened out to the parking lot.

"Did you hear that?" Goody asked his bandmates as he poked his head out of the back door.

They all nodded and pointed up towards the mountains high above them. Goody looked back to where they were pointing, but he couldn't see anything beyond the lights of the parking lot.

There seemed to be a sound, like rushing water. Two of his bandmates, Paul, the saxophonist, and Joe, the drummer, jumped down from the porch behind the restaurant and darted over to where the spotlights were parked. They unhitched the crank that was used to direct the spotlight. The spotlight was hot, so they covered the handles of the spotlight with handkerchiefs, and pointed the light back towards the mountains.

In a moment they all saw a wall of water, 120 feet high, crashing down the mountain towards them.

"Let's try to outrun it. My car's right here," Paul

said.

The bandmates were still piling into the car when the electricity shorted, and all the lights in the nightclub went out.

If they had left only five minutes before, they might have made it. But the car wasn't yet out of the parking lot before it vanished under the water.

The End.

3 OF SOME OTHER METTLE

Not till God make men of some other mettle than earth.
Would it not grieve a woman to be overmaster'd with a piece of
valiant dust?

It was the 20th year after the Great Chastisement.
In general, people had assumed an attitude of normalcy,
although the world was vastly different from what had
been before. The chastisement had killed a huge number
of the world's population, but since then the birthrate had
more than doubled. Cities had been largely abandoned,
and for the present, people preferred to live on farms.

The marvels of the modern age had not been lost
or forgotten, but most people lived simple lives. There
were very few factories because people made most of the
things they needed, or they found those things within
their own villages. People didn't go to movies often, or at
all, preferring to make their own music and entertainment
in local festivals. After the great sign at the end of the
chastisement, there was only one faith. The clergy had not
yet had time to become corrupt, and most everyone went
to Church on Sunday, and on a great many days in

between.

People had gotten past the dreary years of rebuilding what had been lost in the great chastisement, and now most led lives of peace and contentment. It was like the middle ages with plumbing.

There weren't as many career choices as there had been in the past. There were no armies and little need for police. There were local justices to decide a handful of disputes, but there was not a great demand for lawyers. Advertising executives and investment counselors had gone extinct. There were no stocks or exchange-traded funds, or retirement accounts. And most people paid for goods in silver, or in trade.

Most boys grew up to become farmers or tradesmen. Most girls grew up to become wives and mothers. Some boys joined the clergy. The most promising scholars were invited to the universities, which had experienced a profound renaissance. The science of medicine had eliminated almost all diseases, and people were no longer troubled with vaccines and onerous prescriptions.

Some of the girls became religious sisters: some of these joined teaching orders, and some became cloistered. It was one of these cloistered nuns who found herself riding on the back of a horse on a cool evening in June.

Monica gazed at the sun setting into the blue ocean, framed by the crooked outlines of two sparse Carmel pines, and felt sorry for herself. She was riding on the back of a large mare, which was being led by her new husband. They had just been married that morning in the Carmelite Monastery, and were on their honeymoon, camping in the mountains.

Up until that morning, Monica had been a nun in that monastery. She had been happy there. At least she had been happier there than elsewhere. Monica had learned early on that she did not belong in the world. She was different, and she never fit in.

The children in school, especially the other girls were often cruel to her, and they had such vicious thoughts. The boys were nicer when they were younger, but she didn't like playing with boys, and she didn't like boy things. Then when the boys grew older, their minds became filthy and she couldn't bear to be around them.

The monastery had been her only refuge, and now she was leaving it forever. Her thoughts were interrupted when the horse stopped, and she looked down and saw that they had come to the camp for that night. Her husband helped her dismount, and she saw that their spot had already been prepared ahead of time.

The site overlooked the ocean, there was a fire burning, and a fat chicken roasting over it. There was even a spacious tent set up that was large enough to fit a dozen people.

Monica and her new husband did not speak much over dinner. There was also a bottle of wine, but neither of them wanted any, and both went to their beds soon after eating.

The next morning they drank coffee and continued on their journey south. Soon the horse resumed her regular ambling stride, and Monica fell back into her former attitude, rocking with the horse's gentle movements. The air was thick with fog, but her heavy wool poncho kept her warm against the early morning chill.

The smoke rising from the fires around the campground reminded Monica of her childhood in the early years after the great chastisement. In those times, many people lived in camps and slept in tents, and people shared whatever they had to eat. Strangers would come to the camp, and families would take them in, and the strangers would become members of the community.

In the years since then, the earth had yielded great wealth, but people had not forgotten that attitude of generosity and thankfulness. The older people still remembered what had led up to the great chastisement, and they were not anxious to repeat it.

There were still some who lived apart, and who had never joined a village or a family. These people had continued to live alone in the city, as though the chastisement had never happened, and they were thought to be mad by most everyone. They were known as "vandals", and they hid from the eyes of other men, eating mainly canned goods, and watching videos at odd hours. These vandals, (they were mostly men, for it was a very rough life) occasionally turned up near a village doing some crazy, violent thing, and they would usually end up being shot by a farmer defending his family.

There was an order of monks that was devoted to rescuing these vandals from their pitiful life of fear and loneliness. They lived outside year-round, wandering through the country, singing hymns, camping and hunting, and looking for lost souls. They were a brotherhood of rough men, many of whom had formerly been vandals themselves. It was one of these monks who was presently leading Monica's horse: her new husband, Martin.

Monica covered her face and regretted her new life.

She had not been drawn to the religious life so much as repelled by the world. From her earliest memories, Monica could not remember a time when she did not hear two voices: She had normal hearing, through her ears, but she also heard what people thought. It confused her as a child because she thought that everyone could hear the other voice. When she was very young, Monica would talk in the same way that she heard people thinking, as though she were thinking out loud. Her parents thought their child was a little crazy.

As she got older, she began to hear her siblings planning to do things that they should not. And Monica became something of a tattle-tale. And her parents scolded her for doing this.

It wasn't until Monica was 10 years old that her mother finally put it together: that her daughter was hearing their thoughts. It was too fantastic, and her parents worried what the neighbors would say. They took Monica to the priest, and he agreed that they should keep it quiet for fear of how the other children would treat her.

For her part, Monica had always struggled with mistreatment by her peers. When she was younger, the other children thought she was odd. Then when she got older, she learned to hide her talent, but she couldn't help liking or disliking people according to what she heard them thinking. If a girl would think things quite different from what she was saying, Monica would avoid that girl. But it was often that same type of girl who would notice such avoidance, and who would resort to ostracizing and other cruel games.

Monica could hear the children cave into peer pressure and ostracism, and it made her hate them. As she got older, she became more accustomed to the way people thought and acted, but she never could get over hating people for their weakness. Even though she saw the same weakness in herself, she felt powerless to do anything to change. So she tried to be content with her reputation of being strange, and she kept to herself. Her attitude towards the thoughts of others became one of a connoisseur, and she would appreciate and cherish the rare person who possessed great virtue.

When Monica got to be 15, her parents suggested that she join the monastery. She had never thought of becoming a nun, but she decided to give it a try, and she liked it. She did not consider herself to be truly a religious, but the girls there seemed to be more virtuous on average, and she didn't have to worry about being ostracized. Talking and social interaction in the monastery were very limited, so she was less tortured by other people generally. There were still nuns with personality disorders, who would assert themselves in a way similar to what her peers had done when she was a little girl, but this did not work out the same way in her monastery. Those sorts of petty cat-fights would be severely punished by the mother superior, and so Monica was not troubled by them.

The horse stopped, and Martin let Monica know that he was going ahead to make sure the site was ready, and that she should continue on at her present pace. She watched him jog off ahead and missed him only slightly. After a brief pause, she gave the horse a little kick, and she resumed her leisurely gait. Monica did not hate her new husband, but neither did she love him. She was indifferent. His thoughts were not wicked, nor were they particularly virtuous. If she had to describe her new husband's mind, she would say it was boring. It would be like watching a tortoise crossing an immense desert to get to the sea. She could see what path it was going to take, and it wasn't going to be interesting, but rather slow and dull.

Monica wondered how Martin had garnered such a
great reputation among his order of monks. She had
heard in the monastery that her new husband had been
something of a legend, so she was quite unimpressed
when she finally met him. His face was less handsome
than it was rugged. Martin was older than she was, but his
face looked like it had spent all of its existence out of
doors. With such a face, one might expect a personality
full of vigor and charming anecdotes, but instead,
Martin's appeared to be a tall glass of insipid tea. At least
Martin was not a mean person. He seemed to have a
good heart, but he was a far cry from desirable.

Perhaps he had great a fortitude or some other
virtue, apart from his unimpressive intellect. The monks
were all extremely loyal to him. They were even
accompanying Martin and Monica on this trip, following
unseen both in front and behind them. This was why
Monica did not feel apprehensive at the departure of her
new husband. She knew there were dozens of monks
looking after her. Even though she could not read their
thoughts from that distance, she could sense their
presence, and it comforted her.

She imagined that she could get through this.
Monica sighed again and missed her cozy monastery. It
was not that she had been achieving great strides
spiritually, but it was infinitely preferable to being saddled
with a marriage that did not suit her. She was reminded
again of what she had done that had caused the mother
superior to ask her to leave, and it made her face blush.

It was just about two months prior. There had
been a great storm, and the postman, who made weekly
deliveries, had been forced to stay in the guest house.
The mother superior had asked Monica to deliver his
breakfast in the morning. She was supposed to leave the

tray at the door of the guest house, but when she arrived, she felt something powerful drawing her inside. It was early morning and the postman was still asleep in bed, but Monica had never sensed a man who had such a wonderful personality before. It would be difficult to describe the sensation to someone who could not read other's thoughts, but to a connoisseur like Monica, one who had read the minds of thousands, the mind of this postman was truly a rare gem. Hearing his thoughts was like listening to a beautiful piece of music, or like drinking a glass of fine wine.

Monica had lost her sense of self-awareness and had become lost in the thoughts of the postman. He was happily married and had many children, all of whom he loved greatly. Somehow she found herself seated by his head, and stroking his hair. This was not a physical attraction, and Monica was not at all cognizant of what she had been doing. She didn't even know what the postman looked like.

Of course, the postman woke up and was somewhat startled to find one of the cloistered nuns patting his head. It was a great embarrassment, and Monica fled out of the room without saying a word.

She went to her room, and then to the mother superior to confess what she had done. The mother went to the guest house to try and explain, but the postman had already left.

It would have been a great scandal, even though the postman apparently never told anyone of it. Neither did the mother superior. But Monica's confessor and the mother superior decided that this was a warning sign, and that it would be better if Monica left the monastery.

Monica drearily pondered the prospect of returning home, and having to answer all of the questions about why she had been asked to leave. But it wasn't long afterward that the mother superior broached the topic of an arranged marriage to Martin. Monica surprised herself with how quickly she had accepted the proposal, and the wedding was quickly arranged.

Her parents rushed out to the wedding, and both wore bewildered expressions as they watched their cloistered daughter be given away in marriage. Now she was on her honeymoon with a virtual stranger. She wondered if she would ever really get to know such a person. Was it worth it, just to avoid embarrassment?

The horse arrived at the new camp, and Martin came out of the tent to meet them. Everything looked beautiful. Monica noticed that, in addition to the prepared meal of rabbit stew, there also were bouquets of wildflowers throughout the camp.

Martin helped Monica down from the horse, and she noticed that Martin's expression was slightly different. He wasn't thinking anything that would make him feel stressed, but his attitude definitely showed concern.

They had just sat down to eat, when all of a sudden, Martin turned his head, as though he heard a noise.

"Excuse me," he said. He darted off towards a dense thicket at the north edge of the camp, about a hundred yards off. Monica rose to see what was going on, and she saw Martin cautiously approaching the wooded area.

Suddenly a ragged man came out from behind a bush. His hair was long and disheveled, and he wore a crazed expression. Monica had never seen one before, but she recognized him as a vandal from the stories she had heard.

Martin tried to intercept the man, but the vandal seemed like a madman. In his right hand, he held what looked like a knife, and he held a short club in the other. He was swinging both of them about wildly. Martin had no weapon, but held up his open hands in a gesture of peace, trying to calm the man. This had little to no effect, and instead of settling down, the vandal swung his knife at Martin's face. He appeared to miss, or to cut Martin only slightly. Martin attempted to grab the knife away but succeeded only in cutting his hand. Then the club came up and caught Martin on the side of the head, knocking him down.

Then the vandal's eyes turned on Monica, and she became paralyzed with fear. She could sense that his mind was like that of a wild animal. The vandal was filled with fear and hunger, anger and lust.

Once he had Monica in his sights, he sprinted towards her, and Monica was too frightened to even scream. The vandal had covered half the distance to her when Martin lifted his head and rose to one knee. Monica had her eyes fixed on the bloody knife, which was only steps away. Martin lifted his bloody hand and held it out towards the vandal, in what seemed like a last, pitiful attempt to stop the assault on his wife.

Martin's gaze narrowed slightly, and shouted, "No!", and the vandal fell facedown at Monica's feet. Monica looked at her feet, and she could instantly sense that the man was dead. She realized that Martin had used the power of his mind to kill. She turned her eyes to Martin, and then she saw Martin faint and fall over.

Monica had walked back to where the other monks had hidden themselves. They made sure that Martin's wounds were dressed, and then they carried him into the tent. He was not seriously wounded, they said, but the incident appeared to have left him exhausted.

Monica had finally figured things out. The veil had lifted, and Monica saw everything now. Martin could read minds as easily as she could, and moreover, he even had the power to cloud his mind and to hide his thoughts from her. He had been reading her the whole time, ever since they first met.

Martin had sensed the vandal following their party, and he had hoped to catch him before she made camp, but he was not successful. It was only after her life was threatened that Martin had used his mental power to stop the man, and this appeared to have caused an aneurysm of some sort in the brain of the vandal. Martin had never killed anyone before, and the shock of it was too much. He was, after all, a very sensitive soul.

Martin had lived a solitary life, as she had, but he had used his powers to help rescue those lost souls trying to make their way back into society. It was his ability to harness his power to help others that made him legendary among the monks.

Only his confessor knew that Martin could read other's thoughts. Martin had refused to become a priest, but instead had waited, hoping one day to find someone like himself. It was only after hearing about Monica's plight from the mother superior that the arrangement was made.

Monica smiled and thought of how he had tricked her. Martin had a tricky mind, she thought. It was tricky and beautiful. Martin was still unconscious, and she enjoyed studying the fine contours of his personality. He was her husband, she thought, so there was nothing wrong with running her fingers through his hair. So she did this while she studied his thoughts, and watched him sleep.

The End.

STRANGE CAPERS

4 THE BELL INVITES ME

I go, and it is done; the bell invites me.
Hear it not, Duncan, for it is a knell
That summons thee to heaven or to hell.

Guillermo was flying north, towards the family estate. He was wearing a heavy parka, but he dreaded opening the window later. The night was clear with very little wind. It was nearly a full moon. You couldn't ask for a better night. He glanced over to where the rifle was leaning up against the passenger door, but he could barely make it out in the dim light of the cabin.

The estate was high atop Monte Tabor, looking over the Guadalupe Valley and the family vineyard: Bodegas San Simon. Guillermo's father, Tomás, had worked for many years in the Sonoma wine country before returning to his homeland of Mexico. Tomás had taken many prized cuttings back with him. He bought 100 acres in the northern edge of the Guadalupe Valley and dug wells, planted vines, and built the cellar with his own two hands.

Bodegas San Simon was a great success, and Tomás

married a local girl, Maria Theresa. The two raised five children, Tomasito, Roberto, Juan, and the twins, Maria Elena and Maria Dulce. Everyone helped with the vineyard, and the family became very prosperous. The couple couldn't have any more children, and so they decided to adopt. Guillermo was ten years younger than the twins, and he became the baby of the family.

Guillermo always felt different from the other children. He was darker than his brothers and sisters, and the neighboring children always called him 'Indio'. All the older children had married and moved away by the time Guillermo was fifteen, and he was left to take care of the vineyard and his aging parents. Tomás was fifty years older than Guillermo, but Maria Theresa was only 35 years older. Guillermo learned all about the family business, and all of his father's many investments. Hired men now did all of the planting and harvesting, and Guillermo was free to pursue his hobbies of flying, hunting, and horseback riding.

Wild boars had always threatened the vines in the foothills of the estate, and Guillermo had learned to hunt them from his airplane. He would shoot a boar, then fly back to the airstrip in Ensenada, and drive home to San Simone. From there, Guillermo would ride out to the point where the boar lay, bring it back to the estate, and roast the animal on a spit. Guillermo, Tomás, and the workers spent many evenings in the courtyard of their estate, eating roast pork and drinking the family vintage Syrah. The view from atop Monte Tabor was expansive, and at night they could see the lights from Ensenada.

Tomás was very pleased with his youngest son's business acumen, and he had turned over full control of all his interests. This had been a touchy point on a few occasions in the past. Roberto had a small brewery in

Tecate that had run into trouble, and he had asked Tomás for a loan. But Guillermo had counseled against it, as he felt the brewery was too risky. Roberto had to sell his majority share to another party just to keep afloat. Roberto was still angry about that.

Another time, Maria Elena's daughter wanted money to attend a fancy music school in the United States. She had asked Tomás for some money, and Guillermo had informed her that they couldn't afford to waste money on a frivolous education that wasn't in business or engineering. Both of the twins hated Guillermo after that.

When Guillermo turned thirty-five, he decided that he should marry. There was a waitress named Rosa that he knew down in Ensenada. She was always sweet to Guillermo when he came in for breakfast before taking the plane up. Rosa reminded Guillermo of Maria Theresa: she had a certain natural grace and excellent posture. When Guillermo asked her to marry him, she took off her apron and sat down next to him. They were wed a couple of months after that.

And then Tomás died. Because he had seen that Guillermo had been so successful at running the family business, Tomás changed his will so that everything would go to Maria Theresa, and then to Guillermo on her passing. There were some claims that Guillermo had had an undue influence on his father during his declining years, but no one had challenged the will. Not openly.

The twins had visited Maria Theresa more often after Tomás' passing. They didn't include Guillermo or Rosa in any of their plans, often going to the local spa and spending most of their time away from the estate. They never participated in the barbecues in the courtyard.

Tomacito and Juanito had also come to visit a few

times, but they seemed colder, and they spoke less often to Guillermo. Guillermo felt that even his mother was growing more distant from him.

It was nearly a year after Tomás died that Guillermo got a call from the family attorney, Ferdinand. Ferdinand said that Maria Theresa's amended will was ready for her signature. Guillermo told Ferdinand to fax a copy over to him, and that he would look it over with his mother and get back to him after the new year.

Guillermo hung up the phone and was sweating on the back of his neck. The updated will came through the fax, and he quickly read it. The new will would distribute the estate by equal portions to all the children.

Although that seemed fair on the surface, in reality, it ignored all the work that Guillermo had done in improving the family business at the expense of his own career. All the other children had been given help starting their lives away from home, and they had been working on their careers for several decades. Whereas Guillermo had spent his entire life managing the vineyard and his father's investments. The new will was not going to give him any credit for all of that work. He would be left with the same amount the others would be given, but they would get that on top of what they had already earned. It wasn't fair.

Probably the greater source of worry was that, only days before, Rosa had informed him that she was now pregnant with their first baby. Now that Guillermo had a wife and child, he was about to lose everything!

Maria Elena had done this. She had been bad-talking Guillermo to their mother behind his back, and Maria Theresa had been worn down. Maria Theresa had gone to the family attorney and had asked him to undo Tomás' will. Maria Theresa would never have done that on her own. Guillermo was fuming.

Guillermo took the will from the fax and left the house. He drove down to Ensenada and took his plane up. He felt like hunting. He flew back over the vineyard and found a pack of wild boars. He singled one out and imagined that it was his sister. Bam! The boar went down. He had gotten quite good at hunting, and he was able to shoot them through the head with one shot. It was almost too easy.

And then the penny dropped. Guillermo pointed the plane towards the estate on the top of Monte Tabor. Nobody was home. He flew by and examined the courtyard through the rifle scope. It would be easier than hunting boar. But the plane would have to be higher.

He took the plane up another fifty feet and examined the courtyard. It would be night, so he could come at it from any angle without being seen. New Year's was just two weeks away.

The plan was still forming in his head when Guillermo's conscience started to kick in. Could he kill his own mother? Was he some sort of savage?

But she was trying to take away his life's work! All that he had done to provide for his family was going to be stolen away.

And she wasn't his real mother anyway. She had always loved her natural children more. She had just proven that. And she probably only adopted Guillermo to care for her and Tomás in their old age. Like a servant.

Guillermo took the plane back into the canyons and hunted down more boar. Each time he found one, he would say to himself, "If I miss, then I won't do it." But his bullet would hit the boar, through the head, again and again.

Guillermo landed the plane and drove back to the

estate. He couldn't show that he knew. He had to look happy. He barbecued a boar, and served wine, and smiled.

For Christmas Guillermo bought mantillas for his mother and Rosa. Guillermo told Rosa of the tradition where Tomás and Maria Theresa would welcome the new year out in the courtyard. They would toast with a glass of wine and ring the big brass bell at the stroke of midnight.

"Oh let's do that this year," Rosa said eagerly. "We could wear our new mantillas."

Guillermo looked for his mother's approval, and she smiled and nodded yes. Maria Theresa also missed that grand old tradition.

Guillermo was flying an indirect route towards the estate. Even though he would be high above, he didn't want the plane to be visible until the short pass over when he would take his shot. He had left much earlier in the day, explaining to Rosa that he had an important business deal, and that he would be back later in the day. He instructed Rosa that ringing the bell was vitally important, and that she and Maria Theresa must follow through with the plan.

Rosa's mantilla was black and Maria Theresa's was white, providing a clear target at night. Guillermo had also installed a stronger floodlight on the courtyard. Flying over at night on a test run, Guillermo saw that his line of sight would be just as good as if he were shooting in broad daylight.

Another tradition that Guillermo did not need to tell Rosa about, was that every farmer in the surrounding countryside would have a drink and then fire off his rifle at midnight. The hour of midnight would be full of rifle shots, and that is when Guillermo would fire his shot.

One bullet would pierce through Maria Theresa's head, and it would appear to all that she was another innocent victim of that very reckless tradition of celebratory gunfire. Rosa would testify that she heard many rifle shots before Maria Theresa fell. Everyone would figure that it was just a stray bullet, and very bad luck.

It was nearly midnight, and Guillermo set the plane on an easterly course that would put him just above the courtyard as the bell was ringing. Guillermo rolled the window down and the icy air filled the cabin. Rifle shots had already begun to sound in the night, and Guillermo heard the bell striking the first time.

He looked through the scope and saw that Rosa was ringing the bell. Guillermo had left some heavy boxes bear the archway that housed the bell, so that the person ringing the bell would have their view of the valley obscured. Rosa had her back to his plane, and she probably couldn't hear him over the bell.

Guillermo had Maria Theresa in his sights as the bell sounded for the sixth time. This would be his only chance. He thought of the boars he had shot, and he knew it would be just as easy. A small gust of wind jogged the plane just as he squeezed the trigger, and the bell stopped after the eighth ring.

Guillermo watched in horror as his mother ran over to where the body of Rosa lay in the courtyard, but he couldn't watch for long as he needed to stay out of sight. The plane continued eastward until he was well beyond the estate, and then it headed north over the mountains.

The scene below was pitch black. Guillermo flew for a long time, and thought about the wicked thing he had just done: He had murdered his own wife and child! Would Maria Theresa suspect what his plan had been?

Guillermo turned the plane around and headed

towards the airport. He would have to pretend to be shocked. He would stop for a drink and rehearse his reaction in the car. His plan had failed, and now he had to make sure that he wouldn't be caught.

Even though he was over the mountains, he could still hear rifle shots. There was a loud crack of a rifle, and then Guillermo's engine cut out. It was quiet in the cabin now, except for the rush of the cold night air outside. Guillermo tried to restart the engine but failed. Somehow a stray bullet had pierced the gas line. Very bad luck indeed.

The altimeter said that he was up at around 2000 feet, which meant that he could stay aloft only a little more than three miles at the optimum glide ratio. But Guillermo was only a thousand feet over the mountains, and it was all blackness below. He reckoned that the nearest highway, Carretera Federal 3, was ten miles away. There was no way he would have enough time to land the plane safely.

Guillermo wondered about the likelihood of surviving a crash in the mountains, alone in the winter. He glanced over to where the rifle was leaning up against the passenger door, but he could barely make it out in the dim light of the cabin.

The End

5 AS HIS KIND GROW

And therefore think him as a serpent's egg—
Which, hatched, would as his kind grow mischievous—
And kill him in the shell.

Earnest heard the dull thud of his head hitting the tile floor. He coughed once, and then took a deep breath. He heard a door close and opened his eyes. He didn't know where he was, and he didn't remember what had happened before he had fallen asleep. His mind was a complete blank. The room around him was dark, but he could make out the faint outline of the ceiling tile.

He had a memory of gazing up at that ceiling as he lay on a gurney while being wheeled up to a machine...

His head had been fitted into a small chamber, and the pads inside the chamber were brought down upon his head until he was held firmly in place. Then the doctor ... Dr. Guegen asked him a series of questions:

"What is your profession?"

"I'm an engineer by training, although I haven't done it for several years."

"Where did you go to school?"

"CalTech."

"What was the most embarrassing thing that happened to you in school?"

"Do I have to answer that?"

"Not if you don't want to remember …"

Earnest raised his head slowly and looked around the room, and saw that he was alone. There was only one light on, across the room, near the door, and a couple of closets, close by, along the wall. Behind him, Earnest could feel a glass wall. It was warm to the touch, but the room was too dark to see anything inside.   Earnest looked down at the floor and saw that he was wet and naked.

Inside one of the closets, there were several sets of blue scrubs, and he put one on. It was just a pair of loose-fitting cotton pants and a v-neck shirt. Earnest examined himself in the mirror on the closet door and saw that the clothes fit him perfectly.

Earnest looked at his face and saw that he was very fit. He looked to be in his twenties, but Earnest remembered being older than that.

He remembered going to the doctor's appointment. Was it months ago? He had dressed casually in khaki pants and a golf shirt. When he looked at himself in the mirror that morning, he remembered seeing someone paunchier, and with less hair.

He had scheduled the appointment because he had been falling down of late. He had fallen twice just the day previous, when he was out golfing. And his hands would shake when he tried to grip the club.

His wife accompanied him to the doctor's

appointment that morning … (he remembered that he had a wife!) … the doctor ran a series of tests.

He remembered sitting in the office, awaiting the results. The doctor came in looking very sad. Had he been crying? Earnest had known the doctor for many years. The doctor told Earnest that he … was dying? He had brain cancer.

Earnest looked at himself in the mirror again. He didn't look sick. He squeezed his right hand tightly. He felt strong. He could see the veins in his arm. He opened his mouth and saw that he had a good set of teeth. He had a healthy head of black hair.

He closed his eyes and tried to remember. Was this loss of memory from the cancer? He heard the faint ripple of water and saw that it was coming from behind the glass wall.

Earnest felt the urgent need to leave. But why? Perhaps he had an appointment. Maybe his wife would know. But where was she? Esther? He didn't have his phone. Or his wallet.

He knew he had to get out. He felt that his life was in danger. He had to leave right away.

There was a pair of white sneakers in the next closet over, and he slipped them on. He quickly rifled through a series of drawers and found a scalpel. There was an envelope with some cash in it, and Earnest took that too.

Earnest examined himself in the mirror and thought that he could pass for a doctor, or perhaps an orderly. There was a light jacket hanging on the closet door, and Earnest put this on over the scrubs, fitting the scalpel and money into the pockets. He poked his head out of the door and slipped out.

There were no people in the hallway, and Earnest hurried to get away from that room, and out of the building. He remembered walking down that hospital corridor to have his head plugged into the machine. How many times had he done that? It was always the stream of questions picking apart pieces of his memory...

"How was your childhood?"

"Happy, I guess."

"What is your earliest memory?"

"I was in a rocking chair, being held by my grandmother, or somebody."

"How old were you?"

"I don't know. Two?"

"Did you go to pre-school?"

"No. I stayed at home. I was aphasiac when I was young. I couldn't speak until I was 4. My mom says I never said a word until then."

Earnest passed a bank of elevators, and one of them opened.

"Going down?" The lady with strawberry blond hair standing by the door smiled at him, and he smiled back.

Earnest got on the elevator. There were two nurses in lavender scrubs at the rear of the elevator.

"Are you going to the main floor?" the lady asked.

It was at that moment that Earnest realized that he didn't have the power of speech. He understood the lady perfectly, but he couldn't make a reply. He opened his mouth and nothing came out.

The lady gazed at him and cocked her head slightly sideways. Earnest decided that smiling and nodding would suffice, and he did that. He smiled at the two nurses standing at the back of the elevator, and then turned back towards the elevator doors.

"No one ever gets on at the 16th floor. This is a first for me," the lady said.

Earnest smiled and nodded.

One of the ladies behind him said, "They're getting younger and younger."

The elevator door opened again, and the lady looked at Earnest. "This is the first floor," she said.

Earnest stepped out of the elevator. He smiled once again, and beat a hasty retreat.

Without looking for the signs, Earnest walked to the front door of the building. He just wanted to get out. He knew that he would feel safer once he got away.

The green glass door automatically slid open as he approached it, and Earnest instinctively turned right. There was a sidewalk that led to a park, and Earnest followed a dirt path through the park.

It was overcast, and Earnest felt a slight chill from the wind. He was hastily marching through the park without paying attention to the beauty around him. There were trees, green grass, and a lake, and the path before him came to a fork. He chose the path that went to the right, and this led out over a bridge, to a little island in the middle of the lake.

There was a bench nearby, facing the lake, and Earnest sat down on it. He remembered sitting on a bench like that, talking with Dr. Guegen.

"The AI is quite advanced now," Guegen had been saying. "We can take a series of snapshots from your memory, add that to existing pictures, video, and facts surrounding your life, and the AI will do the rest."

"So what do I do?" Earnest asked.

"We'll ask you a battery of questions, and you answer them."

"That's it?"

"Well, we need to plug you into the machine. It's kind of like an MRI. As you use your memory to answer the questions, the computer will take measurements from all the sensory details associated with your memory experiences, and map them out."

Many memories were coming back to Earnest, and he was beginning to feel more normal, but the past was still a jumble. He had been getting treatments for brain cancer, and Earnest reasoned that this had somehow affected his memory. But he didn't yet know what had gone on in that hospital lab, and why he felt the urgent need to flee.

It suddenly dawned on Earnest that he was also going somewhere. Earnest was not merely running away, but he was hastily walking towards something. He was going to meet someone. Who? Was he running into danger? He reached into his jacket and felt the scalpel, and this reassured him, somewhat.

Earnest stood up and walked back toward the path. He came to a high fence with a locked gate and he could not go any further. There was a sign on the gate that said, "DO NOT USE WITHOUT CERTIFIED FACILITATOR".

He remembered meeting Dr. Guegen for the first time. Guegen had shown him a presentation on the current state of cloning.

"We initially start with several clones, and then we freeze all but one. If something goes wrong, we unfreeze another one."

"And how long does it take?" Earnest remembered asking.

Dr. Guegen smiled. "That's the interesting part. If nothing goes wrong, we can bring a clone up to adult size in less than a year."

"And it … he will look like …"

"He will be your perfect genetic twin. Any scars or other injuries that you have, he will not."

Earnest remembered pointing to his lower back. "So this pinched nerve that I have in my back …"

"He won't have any back problems," Dr. Guegen said, "assuming that your pinched nerve isn't a congenital disorder."

Walking along the path, Earnest twisted his back from side to side, and ran for a few steps. His back felt perfectly fine.   He glanced over his shoulder to see if anyone was watching him, but he was alone in the park. He removed the plastic seal from the scalpel and felt the sharp edge with his finger. It cut his finger slightly and he rubbed the blood between his thumb and finger. Earnest put the scalpel back into his pocket.

On the other side of the park was an elevated rail platform, and Earnest climbed up the stairs towards the northbound train. There was a ticket machine, and he put a bill in and pushed a button. A ticket dropped out, and Earnest retrieved it without bothering to collect his change.

Several people were waiting on the platform, and Earnest stood aloof, mimicking their same attitude. A vagrant who frequented that station filched the change from out of the ticket machine, and then approached Earnest to see if there was more where that came from.

"Hey man," the vagrant said.

Earnest didn't respond, and the vagrant took a stance with his face just two feet from Earnest's ear. "Hey man," the vagrant said.

Earnest turned his head and looked into the vagrant's eyes.

"Could you spare a couple of bucks?" the vagrant asked. He was a few inches taller, and about fifty pounds heavier than Earnest.

Earnest smiled at the vagrant and turned his head back towards the el track.

The vagrant tugged on Earnest's sleeve. "Hey man, I asked you a question."

Earnest waved his hand in the vagrant's face. The vagrant balled his fists for a moment, and then noticed that other people on the platform were looking at him. He thought better of it and walked away.

The train pulled in soon after, and Earnest took a seat at the front corner of the car. The doors closed, the train pulled away, and Earnest looked over at the map of the el train. He watched the different colored lines intersect on the map at the various stops, and he saw the stop at which he had to get off. That was where he lived.

Another memory suddenly came back. It didn't seem that long ago. Earnest remembered hearing the good news from the doctor. His cancer had been cured! He had counted himself out long before. The cloning had been the desperate act of a man with very little time, and too much money.

Dr. Guegen had been skeptical about the news. "Are you sure?" he asked.

"Gee, try not to be too excited, Doc," Earnest had said.

"The cancer prognosis was very grim," Guegen replied. "You had less than a year."

"I know, it's crazy," Earnest shrugged. "But it's true. My cancer doctor's one of the best. He was using neutron therapy."

"So, what do you want to do?"

"That's what I wanted to ask you. I've been coming here for months now, pouring my memories into that thing."

"It's not a thing," Dr. Guegen said. "That's you. He's almost finished."

"That's not me," Earnest had said. "I'm me."

"You wouldn't be able to convince him of that. He looks like you. He has your memories. You should come to the lab and see him."

"I told you that would just freak me out. Can't we just pull the plug?" Earnest suggested.

"And throw all that work down the drain?" Dr. Guegen sounded upset. "What if you have a recurrence? It happens, you know."

Earnest nodded. "I guess you're right. We don't have to decide right now. I only have a few more scheduled visits anyway."

"That's right," Guegen said. "If you decide to terminate the project, we can just stop the heart before he becomes conscious. Are you ready to go?"

Earnest sat bolt upright on the train, remembering. His forehead was covered in sweat despite the cool cabin of the train. The memory of the conversation filled him with fear. Perhaps it was that fear that woke him prematurely, and which caused him to flee from the tank in the lab.

He looked up at the subway map again, and then

his eyes went beyond to the next stop, and the next. His eyes wandered up to the top of the map, and he speculated briefly about continuing on the train. What if he should stay on until the end of the line.

But after a moment's reflection, it didn't seem like a plausible alternative. If he didn't go home, he had no idea of where he would find food or shelter. He had no ID or credit card, and only a little money. Could he just run away, and perhaps become a farmhand somewhere?

The train bumped along and Earnest was oblivious to the clatter, or to anything else inside the train. The city outside the window grew more dense, the buildings taller, and signs appeared on the platform, telling passengers about educational opportunities that awaited them if they enrolled now. But Earnest did not read about the opportunities as he waited patiently for his stop.

After thirty minutes, Earnest got out of his seat and stood near the exit before the train informed him that he was at Adams and Wabash, and that he could transfer to the orange, pink and brown line trains, if he was a mind to.

Earnest left the train and scrambled down the stairs, as if he had been taking this route for years. Once he was down at the street level, he continued north for about two minutes and then entered a large, glass high-rise.

He took the elevator to the 72nd floor, and soon found himself at the door of the east, south, and north-facing penthouse condominium. Earnest pulled the scalpel out of his jacket pocket, and without even thinking, he entered the five-digit security code on the pad and opened the front door.

Earnest entered the condominium apartment and

was not even slightly impressed by the view of the harbor. His hand still held the scalpel, but it swung at his side as he walked through the kitchen and living room, looking for the man who wanted to kill him.

There was a large oak door that led into the library, and it was here that Earnest found the man. The man was seated with his back to the door, and a blue sweater hung loosely over his hunched shoulders.

Earnest did not try to sneak up on the man, but walked towards him with the vague intent of pleading for his own life, without the capacity of speech. The man turned around and was startled by seeing Earnest. His hands were shaking as he attempted to stand hurriedly, pushing up with his right hand on the reading table, and his left hand on his chair.

The face looking at Earnest's was his own face: the face he remembered having. But the man's eyes were filled with fear.

"You!" the man said in a weak shout. The man's eyes went down to the scalpel that Earnest held at his side, and he rushed to stand behind the desk near the back of the room.

Earnest saw that he was scaring the man, and so he laid the scalpel on the desk and held up his hands to reassure him. Earnest took a seat in the chair opposite.

The man pulled the scalpel over to his side of the desk and sat down.

"I don't know why you're here. I guess you think you live here. Don't you?" the man said.

Earnest shook his head. He had already realized that he was the clone, and that the man sitting across from him was the real one.

"You were a mistake. You shouldn't even be alive now. You know that, right?"

Earnest nodded.

"So then, what did you come here for?"

Earnest couldn't answer even if he could talk. He had wanted to live. That's why he had run away, and he thought he could plead now with the man whose memories he shared.

"Did you want money? That's what you wanted, isn't it? That's what everyone wants."

The man turned his back on Earnest, and Earnest's turned his eyes downward, and he contemplated the oak wood floor. The sure knowledge that his memories were not his own suddenly gave him perspective. He was able to distance himself from things he had said and done in the past. He no longer had to justify anything he had done, and he could see those actions for what they truly were. Earnest raised his head and looked at the man across from him, and realized what a selfish, petty, mean, and spiteful person he was. He could never hope to expect any compassion from that man.

The man turned around and glared at Earnest. "Why are you smiling?" the man asked.

Earnest could only shake his head.

"I never signed up for this. You can't expect me to provide for you. You're just a clump of my cells. I thought I was going to die, but I'm not. I'll bet you're sorry about that."

Earnest thought about the man's many misdeeds: the shady business deals, the lies, the selfishness, and the cruelty. It made Earnest glad that he was not the man who had lived the life of those memories.

He was lost in thought for a moment, and he did not notice that the man had moved behind him. The last thing Earnest heard was the crack of a marble statuette on the back of his head.

The man, whose name was Earnest Böse, was talking on the phone with Dr. Guegen.

"He's on the floor. No, he isn't dead. Yet. I just gave him a crack on the back of the head. How the hell did he get down here anyway? …. My memories. Right. That's obvious now. I'm still a little shaken up. I mean, he just appeared out of nowhere. That freaked me out. But look, Doc, you gotta make this guy disappear. Pronto. You said that he was never going to wake up. … Look, I'll tell you what to do. You come down here, and call an ambulance for your patient. You ride back to the hospital with him and … take care of him down there. … I don't care what you do with him. Freeze him. Put him back in the tank. You can sell his organs for research. I don't care. Just get him out of my sight."

Earnest Böse looked at the statuette he was holding in his hand. "Oh, look. Now I got blood on my award."

Böse left the library to find a towel to clean the statue. "Listen Doc, you know the code, just let yourself in. I'll be here."

He walked towards the bathroom to get a towel, and then he heard something clatter in his office. He opened the door to investigate, and he saw that a large vagrant was ransacking the apartment. "What are you doing? How did you get in here?"

The vagrant ran at Böse, who was suddenly frightened, and turned to flee. "Help!" Böse said.

But Earnest Böse had a pinched nerve in his back that prevented him from being able to run, and the vagrant easily caught him.

"I told you I just needed a couple of bucks," the vagrant said.

Several months later, Earnest was sitting across from Dr. Guegen in the doctor's office. The cancer was still in remission, and months of speech therapy had almost completely restored his ability to talk. The memory of waking up on the floor of the library still bothered him, though.

"It's quite understandable that the brain cancer affected your speech," Dr. Guegen said.

"But I was aphasiac as a child," Earnest said. "You don't think that's related?"

"It might be, but I don't see how that's relevant to your treatment." Dr. Guegen was studying Earnest's chart. "It seems that you're almost back to normal," he said.

Earnest hesitated for a moment, and then asked: "I'm still a little fuzzy about the past, Doc. Exactly what did you do for me? I mean, what was your capacity in my treatment?"

Dr. Guegen regarded Earnest casually. "I took on the role of preserving any of your memory that was lost due to the cancer treatments."

"I have this memory of you asking me questions, and hooking me up to a machine ..."

"Yes. That really happened. You recorded all of your memories just in case they were lost."

Earnest nodded. He regarded Dr. Guegen sheepishly. "There's one other thing. I know this sounds crazy, but ... did you make a clone of me?"

Dr. Guegen suppressed a small smile. "There was one visit, early on, where you asked me to clone you in case you died. But I told you that I don't have the ability. I don't believe anyone has. Maybe you just had a dream about that, and the dream was confused for reality. The memory is a very delicate thing."

"But I feel so much younger now," Earnest said. "I don't have any grey hair, and my back feels perfect."

"That's quite normal. You were looking at a very real possibility of death, and now you've recovered. You have a new lease on life. Don't feel guilty over that. Just be grateful."

Earnest nodded, and he left the office feeling a little more assured.

After the door closed, Dr. Guegen opened a file cabinet and found a thick file. He took the contents out of several folders and incorporated them into a single unnamed folder. Guegen then moved the unnamed folder into a hidden office safe, which he carefully locked.

The End

STRANGE CAPERS

6 AND SOMETIME VOICES

Be not afeard; the isle is full of noises,
Sounds, and sweet airs, that give delight and hurt not.
Sometimes a thousand twangling instruments
Will hum about mine ears; and sometime voices,
That, if I then had waked after long sleep,
Will make me sleep again: and then, in dreaming,
The clouds methought would open, and show riches
Ready to drop upon me; that, when I waked,
I cried to dream again. yet for aught I see, they are as sick that
surfeit with too much as they that starve with nothing.

Edgar received the message from James Branigan
via courier. Branigan had always carried out his business
in this way. He didn't trust the postal service, and he
knew his phones would likely be bugged.

The message was brief: Susan, his wife, had been
acting strangely, ever since he had given her a bracelet.
The courier had also brought the bracelet in a separate
parcel, still in a box.

The message requested that Edgar examine Susan
at Branigan's yacht, which was presently moored in

Boston.

Edgar had known Branigan long before Branigan had become a most eligible bachelor and a household name. They had gone to the same prep school, Xavier High, in New York. Branigan, the scion of a real estate magnate, was a big personality even then. He was the life of the party, the captain of the swim team, and all the girls in the sister school, St. Chapin, openly fought over his attention.

Edgar had known Branigan from the swim team. They were good friends, although Edgar was more of a shy academic. They kept in touch throughout the years. Edgar had gone on to a career in naval intelligence and was now a psychiatrist in Boston.

Edgar canceled his afternoon appointment and walked down to the pier. He took a circuitous route. Edgar knew that Branigan did not want it to get out that his wife was seeing a psychiatrist. Susan had probably taken an indirect route to the harbor as well. Branigan also used doubles, so the media probably thought that she was currently shopping in New York.

Security let Edgar pass through quickly. They had his photo and had been expecting him. Branigan's yacht had a large common room below deck. Susan was waiting for him there, smoking a long thin cigarette, and drinking coffee. She smiled and stood up to greet Edgar.

"I know you were at our wedding, but we didn't really get a chance to talk," she said, holding out her hand. "I'm Suzy."

Edgar shook her white-gloved hand. Everything about Susan was perfect. She wore a knee-length skirt that was brown for fall, and most likely an original that had been designed for her. Not a hair was out of place.

Susan and Branigan had married five years prior. It was a media event, and they now had two children together.

"Did Bran …. I mean, did James tell you what this was about?" Edgar asked.

Susan looked down, slightly ashamed. "Jimmy told me that you were a psychiatrist. I don't think I would have come if you weren't a family friend, but I honestly do not know why he insisted on this visit. I mean, I feel fine. I'm not depressed or anything. I've never even seen a psychologist before."

She smiled at Edgar, perhaps to demonstrate that she was, indeed, very happy.

"Well, I'm sorry to have to put you through this," Edgar said. "I'm sure James would not have arranged this if he wasn't concerned."

"Oh, Jimmy wanted me to give you this." She fetched a sealed envelope out of her purse and handed it to Edgar.

Edgar opened the letter.

"Give her the box," it said.

Edgar took the jewelry box out of his pocket and handed it to Susan. Her eyebrows went up in surprise.

"What is this? Is this some sort of game Jimmy arranged?"

She took the box and smiled, opening it. Inside was a gold bracelet, featuring what appeared to be a jaguar, fashioned out of jade.

Susan squealed with delight when she saw it. "A jaguar! I love it. Jimmy knows I love jaguars."

Edgar had already examined the box beforehand. He had discovered that Jimmy had wired the box to a nine-volt battery that would deliver a slight electric shock when someone grasped the bracelet. Jimmy liked to play jokes like that.

Edgar watched as Susan grasped the bracelet and got shocked. He had expected that she would pull her hand away and make some reaction of fright or shock, but Susan did none of those things. She held on to the bracelet, and then fixed her gaze upon Edgar. Her eyes appeared to roll up into her head, so that for a brief moment, he only saw the whites of them. Then her irises reappeared and she refocused upon him.

"072829-Jaguar," she said.

"Branigan is right," Edgar thought. "She is acting strangely."

Susan had always struck Edgar as having some sort of affectation. Whenever he heard her giving interviews on television, she spoke with a strange mid-Atlantic accent, with soft r's, and strange vowel sounds that might come from Brooklyn or New Orleans. Seeing her in a trance-like state was not as strange to Edgar as one might have thought, because Susan had always struck him as having a personality somewhat like that of a marionette.

There was a definite history of being hypnotized at some point in her past, but Edgar was not able to discern who had done it.

Branigan had probably suspected as much, and he had chosen Edgar to examine because of his intelligence background.

For his part, Edgar had some experience with a test subject who had been involved in mind control experiments, but his knowledge of those programs was somewhat limited.

Although Susan had been reduced to a trance-like state,

the secrets of her history were still hidden to him, and Edgar no way of finding the code words necessary to uncover that part of her past:

> "Who do you talk to?"
> "I'm talking to you right now," Susan said.
> "What are your orders?"
> "You haven't given me any orders."

There were hints that Susan had undergone some type of trauma-based mind control: When he began to pry about her past hypnotic   experiences, Susan started to develop visible welts around her wrists, as though there she had been held by tight restraints. She also seemed to give him a sort of warning about prying into her programming:

> "Did you know that I have a bomb wired into my belly? If it is disturbed, the bomb might go off."

The welts around her wrists gave Edgar a deep concern for Susan's well-being, and he thought it would be better not to go too deeply all at once. Rather than subject her to further trauma, he gave her a suggestion that she should sleep. He then counted down from ten, and Susan slept deeply.

Susan awoke with no memory of the bracelet, or of what had happened. She glanced about her, remembering where she was.

"Well, this is awkward," she said, stretching.

"It's very common for patients to fall asleep during a visit," Edgar lied. "It shows that you have a peaceful conscience."

Susan resumed a more confident demeanor. "I told James there was nothing wrong," she said.

"I might want to see you for another visit. I'll let you know," Edgar said. "Until then, tell James that you need to catch up on your sleep."

Susan held out her hand to shake Edgar's. "Now that's the kind of prescription I like," she said.

Susan smiled and waved goodbye as she left, and Edgar listened as she climbed the stairs, back up to the main deck.

Branigan's father had done a background check on Susan before James had married her, but Edgar examined the file and found it to be superficial, with large gaps of time unaccounted for. Despite those insufficiencies, there were still some parts of her story that stood out. For example, Susan had been raised in all-girls schools until attending the Sorbonne, and George Washington University; and her physical activities were limited to volleyball, dance, and horseback riding. Yet there was an incident, just before they had been married: a photographer had been harassing Susan in New York, and she had judo flipped him onto the pavement! Did she learn Judo at the Sorbonne?

There were also some items in Susan's bio that made Edgar suspect that she had ties to intelligence agencies: Susan was fluent in four languages; Her father had gone to Yale, and he was a member of a secret society. Edgar knew several people in the intelligence service, who had also gone to Yale, and who belonged to the same society. Certainly, it was not proof, but it bore looking into. Susan's step-father was also very close to several men who held very high positions in the intelligence service.

Finally, Edgar noticed that Susan's childhood riding instructor, DeGuzman, was a foreign national with intelligence ties. Edgar recognized the name, and knew him to be closely associated with another man that Edgar believed was an assassin. Again, this could all be a coincidence, but Edgar needed to investigate further. He assigned the case to a detective that he trusted, and who would be discreet. Edgar also arranged a meeting with Purdy, a fellow he knew from naval intelligence who might give him more insight into the case.

Purdy didn't like it that Edgar had used the phone, even if it was just to arrange a meeting time. A week later they were having hot dogs on a bench, looking out on the Charles River. Edgar gave Purdy a brief rundown, leaving the names out.

"This is very bad for your friend," Purdy said.

"How so?"

"Jaguar, cougar, panther … these are all MK-Ultra assassination profiles. Jaguar usually means foreign assignments."

"Well, then she's safe in-country, right?"

"Not necessarily," Purdy said. "It's just a designation. But the stone is also bad," he said.

"Jade?"

"Jade means she's already done two assignments. She's a professional killer."

"You're kidding. This kid is harmless. She knows how to do embroidery."

"It doesn't matter what her personality seems to be. These people are mind-controlled. Once they have been activated, they're not even aware of what they do."

Edgar wanted to read the detective's background

report before sending a message to Branigan. Edgar received the report on Thursday afternoon, and he stayed late in his office reading it. The report confirmed his suspicions. There were photocopies of two letters written by Susan near the time of her graduation from George Washington University. She was writing to potential employers that she would not be able to accept their internship because she had been offered a job at the CIA. The point she began working at the CIA coincided with an era of her life that had not previously been accounted for.

The background report showed that, after her internship at the CIA, she took a job as a photographer for a national news magazine. Soon after, Susan left for a photo assignment in an Eastern European country that was undergoing a regime change. When that assignment was finished, she started another assignment in a country in the West Indies that was also undergoing a regime change. Edgar wondered if that was when Susan had earned her 'jade' status.

She returned stateside and was given the job of photographing the very eligible bachelor, James Branigan. They were married the following year.

There was also a sort of post-script on the report, dealing with Susan's most recent history. She had been treated for migraines and depression, which began around the same time that she had started with the CIA. The prescriptions she had been given were pretty heavy duty.

The last item was strange for its brevity: Susan had had a miscarriage just four months prior. It seems that she had spent a month recuperating, away from Branigan, on the yacht of a foreign billionaire, who had ties to international drug cartels and intelligence services.

There was no telling what went on during that

yachting excursion. Edgar hadn't heard anything about it in the news.

Edgar started to write a note to Branigan. It was nearly seven o'clock at night, and he was the only one in the office. After getting halfway down the page, Edgar decided to bring the news to Branigan personally. If he left now, he could make the nine o'clock flight. Edgar called a cab, packed the report into his valise, and grabbed his heavy coat. Then he heard glass breaking just outside of his office door.

James Branigan thought it was odd that Edgar had not yet tried to contact him. Susan had gone to see Edgar two times, and he had not responded at all.

Susan's behavior had made Branigan very concerned. Just three days ago he had found her, at about three in the morning, standing in the middle of the bedroom, holding the phone receiver. There was a blank expression on her face, and she hadn't recalled anything about it the next day. Branigan had hoped that Edgar could get to the bottom of all this. He cared a great deal about Susan, but he couldn't afford a scandal.

There was a knock at the door.

"Come in," Branigan said.

It was Van Meter from the secret service. "Mr. President, the first lady is in the car, and she asked me to tell you that she has been waiting for fifteen minutes."

President Branigan stood up and caught his reflection in the mirror near the door. He quickly straightened his tie and ran a hand through his thick brown hair.

Susan smiled at Branigan as he sat down next to her, and the presidential limo started away.

"Sorry to keep you waiting," Branigan said. "I was trying to reach … somebody."

"That's all right, dear," Susan said. She looked very stylish, dressed in a new green wool skirt suit with a matching pillbox hat. She scooted over closely to Branigan, and gently hooked her arm with his. Branigan liked the smell of her perfume.

The End.

7 A LOCAL HABITATION AND A NAME

And as imagination bodies forth
The forms of things unknown, the poet's pen
Turns them to shapes and gives to airy nothing
A local habitation and a name.
Such tricks hath strong imagination,
That if it would but apprehend some joy,
It comprehends some bringer of that joy.

     Sylvia had been digging in the garage for over a
week, and she had eliminated most of the pile of
memorabilia that had accumulated over thirty years of
marriage. Their youngest had left for college in the fall,
and now the perpetual excuse of not having enough time
had also vanished.
     Both Sylvia and her husband Rob were packrats,
with an innate fear of being in desperate need of
something, just after having thrown it away. They had
bought the house soon after they were married, and the
extra boxes of memories, books, and old papers were
settled into the far corner of the three-car garage. The
initial trove in the corner soon spread out along the far

wall, where old computers and defunct electronic gadgets were soon hidden by boxes of old clothes, textbooks, and magazine subscriptions. Occasionally, something old could be fished out of the pile, and the fear of tossing away something useful would be once again affirmed. But just as often, the needed thing could not be found under the mountain of chattels. Before too long, the three-car garage had become a two-car garage; and before their youngest had left, it was impossible to exit out of the right rear passenger door.

But now Sylvia had made a plan and was carrying it out. She had mercilessly given away years of old clothes and books, and had thrown years and years of magazine subscriptions into the recycling bin. The more she worked, the more the spell of the fearful hoarder had been broken, and the luster of many goods had worn off. Now Sylvia would often look into a box, and wonder why she or Rob had ever found any value in it.

The only exception was the papers. Sylvia could not read every paper she found, and she didn't want to destroy or lose whatever memory or property that was recorded on some random, aged sheet of paper. So she had adopted the tactic of scanning everything, and then filing the electronic document on the computer, under whatever category was suggested by the other documents in the box.

This method had been very successful, and she had managed to free up vast portions of the garage that had not seen the light of day in decades. It was very empowering. Sylvia imagined that she was like a pirate, slashing and burning through the remnants of the weak and decaying garage civilization, that could no longer sustain or defend itself: Old exercise equipment that had been intended to preserve health and fitness, and which had never been used; once trendy clothes that now looked garish; and formerly indispensable adaptors and dongles that were no longer even recognizable.

Her work was also like that of an archeologist: as she made progress, the possessions revealed progressively older eras of her family's life. The outer layer contained books and clothes from her children's high school years. Underneath that, there were children's art projects from elementary school. Beneath that, she found boxes of baby clothes and a mobile of cartoon insects.

Finally, she had uncovered the original cache in the far corner of the garage. These were the files that Sylvia and Rob could not part with when they first moved into the house. It consisted mainly of a file cabinet and several banker boxes of files. Sylvia remembered the old university days when she and Rob were graduate students working in cognitive science.

Sylvia opened one of the boxes and read from the first pages that described an experiment in "data translation". The official title of their study was "investigating information processing in biologically-realistic neural networks." Sylvia vaguely remembered that their studies had involved the biological process for recording and indexing memories. It was a cutting-edge study at the time, and they were working under a very generous professor who had many academic credentials next to his name.

Sylvia read from the descriptive page of the first file: "The object of this study is to determine if a subject will recognize and record programming code as organic memories. The subject will assimilate memories that are purely external and invented by another."

It sounded interesting, but her initial response was that the study must have failed, because if it had succeeded, she surely would have remembered it. In cleaning the garage, it had been Sylvia's practice to create a file name on the computer and begin feeding the papers into the scanner at this point, but this study had attracted her attention, and she kept on reading to discover the outcome.

The test subject was interviewed before the experiment, and it was determined that he had never been to Europe, but that he had wanted to go. The subject was familiar with many of the major landmarks from pictures and movies he had seen, and he could recognize them without any coaching.

Next, a series of statements were created which described seeing the various landmarks for the first time. Sylvia glanced over the statements, which recited the minute details that a tourist might experience. The descriptions did not stray far from the mundane, as if they had been lifted from the most prosaic travel guide:

"... 15. I stood underneath the Eiffel Tower and looked up.   16. I took the elevator to the top of the Eiffel Tower.

17. I had lunch at the top of the Eiffel Tower.

18. I watched the boats down below, in the Seine River...."

The list of statements went on for many pages, as would be necessary to describe the details of visiting several landmarks. Certain key details were underlined as unique identifiers. These were made to ensure that information recorded was from the experimental input, and not merely an invention of the test subject.

After this, the statements were translated into a series of electronic stimuli. The subject returned to the lab and was hooked up to a harness that delivered the stimuli to the appropriate areas of the brain. The subject was then given a sedative. The actual delivery of the stimuli took less than five minutes, but the subject was asleep for more than two hours. The subject was then sent home.

In the last phase of the experiment, the subject was interviewed again, and was questioned about any experience with European travel. Interestingly, in the second interview, the subject responded that he had been to Europe. He didn't seem to remember that he had previously answered in the negative. The subject went on to describe visiting several points of interest in Europe, traveling on the route that had been outlined in the experimental description. The key details were given freely by the subject, or when prompted by the experimenter.

The subject didn't appear to have any idea that the memories were not his own, and as expected, he filled in and invented details that the programmed description had left out.

One curious note left by the experimenter concerned the pronunciation of the Eiffel Tower. In the first interview, the subject pronounced it "EYEFUL", as a normal English speaker would. But in the second interview, he pronounced it "EFF-ELLE", as a Frenchman would.

Sylvia was still reading the study when the garage door opened and Rob returned. They ate take-out Chinese food with a bottle of wine, while Sylvia described the study to Rob.

"And the test subject repeated all of the key phrases?" Rob asked.

"That's right. He repeated the same vintage of the wine that he drank. He named the same airline. He stayed in the same hostel…"

"That's fascinating," Rob said. "Was it repeated?"

"You don't remember working on this study?" Sylvia asked.

"No," Rob said. "But that was a long time ago. We were graduate students 30 years ago."

"I guess," Sylvia said.

Rob took a sip from his wine. "You know, this reminds me of my trip to Europe," he said. "It was the summer between college and graduate studies. I remember going to France and visiting the Eiffel Tower…"

Sylvia's ears perked up. While she had heard him say "Eiffel Tower" before, this was the first time she remembered Rob pronouncing it "EFF-ELLE".

The next day, Sylvia scanned the first case study to her computer, and then went back to the file cabinet to read the next case file. Rob's comments the night before made her wonder if he had been the subject of the previous study, but she did not bring it up with him. Perhaps she and Rob had used each other as test subjects those many years ago. The machinery and techniques were all new, and they may have wanted to make sure that the experiment was safe to use before trying it out on the general public. It was still curious that neither of them remembered the experiment.

The preface to the next study acknowledged the success of the previous European travel experiment, and now sought to replace previously recorded preferences with other ones set by the experimenter. The goal was not to remake all of the subject's tastes, but just a select few.

The subject was questioned about a wide variety of his tastes regarding food, clothes, fashions, etc…:

"….18. What is your favorite color?

19. What kinds of foods do you like?

20. What kinds of foods do you hate?…"

The subject was also asked about any allergies, or other medical necessity to avoid certain foods or fabrics.

The subject in this study stated that she loved, among other things, steak, and that she did not like avocados. The subject's favorite color was blue, and the favorite author was Raymond Chandler.

As before, a script was prepared, but this time, there was much less time devoted to the information to be input. Sylvia noted that the entirety of statements fit onto one page:

"…3. I like avocados….

7. I do not like steak…

9. My favorite color is green….

11. My favorite author is Jane Austen."

This was translated into stimuli. Again, the subject was given a sedative and fitted with the electronic headgear. The subject slept for several hours, but the actual transmission took less than a minute.

A few days later, the subject was questioned regarding foods, authors, and fashions. The answers were all the same, as previously given, except now the subject liked avocados, the color green, and all the other likes and dislikes implanted by the experiment.

Sylvia was shocked. In less than a minute, the subject's tastes were involuntarily switched, without her having noticed or even caring in the slightest!

Sylvia also noticed that all of the items that the subject had been "taught" to like or dislike, were things that she currently liked and disliked. Had she been the subject of the second experiment?

As with the previous study, neither the

experimenter nor the subject was named; and to her knowledge, the experiment was only run one time.

The next file was much shorter and did not contain a hypothesis or even a description of the methodology. Instead, there was only a script, which one might assume was translated and then fed into the mind of a sleeping subject:

"23. When I first saw MYLOVE, my heart was beating rapidly....

26. I felt at that instant that MYLOVE and I were destined to be together forever....

35. Working in the lab with MYLOVE was a dream come true....

42. I made my mind up that MYLOVE and I should be married..."

Sylvia could not read anymore. She felt that she had been tricked. It was one thing to change her tastes as part of an experiment: she probably had agreed to the major outline of that experiment beforehand. But this was going too far!

Had her relationship with Rob been part of a scheme? Did she fall in love and marry Rob because of a script that had been subconsciously implanted in her brain?

When Rob got home, Sylvia raised the topic of the taste experiment. Rob was as surprised to hear about it as she had been.

"So the subject just stopped liking whatever he liked, and switched to liking something else?"

"Yes. Or whatever she liked," Sylvia suggested, trying to introduce the topic of how she had been wronged.

"Oh, was it a she?" Rob asked.

"I don't know," Sylvia admitted. "None of the subjects are named, of course."

"Do you know which one of us performed the experiment?" Rob asked.

"No. I don't remember anything about it, and the paperwork doesn't give any clues."

"Hmm," Rob pulled on his chin, trying to solve the riddle. "Well, what did the subject end up liking?"

"Avocados," Sylvia said.

"I like avocados," Rob said.

"So do I," Sylvia emphasized, hoping that Rob would pick up on what she was suggesting. "And the color green became her favorite color."

"That's my favorite color and yours," Rob said. "What else?"

"Jane Austin became her favorite author."

"We both like Jane Austin," Rob said.

Sylvia didn't say anything more. She couldn't prove that she had been wronged until she had more evidence.

It was a fitful night for Sylvia. She had terrible dreams. One of them involved her walking a tiger on a leash. When she awoke, she was filled with a sense of dread.

Rob had already left, so she went down to the garage, and dove into the pile of papers and books in the corner. She remembered that the professor had given her and Rob credit in some of his textbooks. Sylvia opened the books, one by one, and scanned the title pages. In every one, she could see her name in the acknowledgments, but Rob's was nowhere to be found.

Memories kept coming back to her, as they had in glimpses in her dreams. She remembered working in the lab with the professor, and she remembered writing up studies and translating the stimuli. But she had no memory of working with Rob as a colleague in the lab.

The memory of when she had first met Rob had only just come back to her last night. She had a memory of when he first entered the lab. He was answering an ad seeking volunteers for experiments. Rob was also a graduate student, but he was working in Electrical Engineering and Computer Science.

Her newfound memories were embarrassing to her, but they seemed like they were real. Sylvia remembered that it was she whose heart had fluttered when she first saw Rob. Rob had been the subject of the first study, and Sylvia thoroughly enjoyed working with Rob in the interview process: He was so confident and self-assured. Sylvia was so pleased with herself when she had been able to implant memories into his mind. It gave her a great sense of power.

Sylvia never reported the results to her advisor. She kept them to herself, and she invited Rob back for a second experiment. Rob was only too happy to oblige. It was easy money for a grad student to make on the side, for just a few hours of his time.

Perhaps the idea had been in her mind from the very beginning, or maybe it had just grown through the experimental process. But after the second experiment, it became clear that Sylvia could make Rob her own if she wanted to.

During the interview process, it came out that Rob already had a girlfriend. Sylvia didn't consider herself to be bad-looking, but she didn't kid herself into thinking that she could win men over with her looks. Also, she had always been a little on the shy side, so she didn't feel that she could exert any charm over Rob either. But the experiments had shown that the girlfriend would be of no consequence after some careful programming.

Rob's attitude towards her changed after the last experiment, and she hid all of the results. She claimed that the results had been a failure, and her advisor allowed Sylvia to change the focus of her dissertation.

There was one last program that she ran on herself, which gave Sylvia the false memory that she and Rob had worked together in the lab. They both had the same memory, and there had never been any reason to check. Until now. The acknowledgments in the book proved that her current memories were the correct ones.

Sylvia was left with a deep aching sense of loss.

When Rob came home that evening, he found Sylvia busy shredding files. Sylvia was crying.

"What's wrong, babe?" Rob said, stroking her shoulder.

Sylvia felt his hand, and she thought of how she had programmed him to love her, and this made her feel even worse.

"It's just the memories ... all the time. It's all gone," she said.

"That's alright," Rob said. "We still have each other."

The End

8 IN SEQUENT TOIL

Like as the waves make towards the pebbled shore,
So do our minutes hasten to their end;
Each changing place with that which goes before,
In sequent toil all forwards do contend.

It was during the war, and I was in uniform, so I fit right in. I felt a little guilty that I was wearing an army officer's uniform, even though I have never been in the army.

I consoled myself with the thought that I was an agent of the Historical Review Board, which was kind of like being an officer in the armed forces. I was even more powerful than a mere army captain.

The atmosphere in the club was quite lively as I entered: everywhere I looked there were young sailors and army, dancing and cavorting with young ladies, while popular music blared from the full orchestra on the stage. I noticed the violation right away: the current year was 1943, but the song had been written in the 1980s, and rearranged for a "big band" sound. This was what had triggered the alarm, and my investigation.

I looked at the stage, and that was when I first laid eyes on Alba. Her name had been prominently featured on the billboard outside. She had a beautiful voice, and she sang the song without any of the flourishes and gimmicks that other singers often use to cover over their lack of talent. Her most striking feature was her large, brown eyes. Alba looked to be in her early twenties, but her eyes looked like they had seen much more of life than that. I noticed that Alba sang with impeccable rhythm and a very thick Portuguese accent. Although I had come to the club strictly on business, I suddenly found myself more than a little distracted.

I had come to the 88 Club in New York to investigate the theft of intellectual property by Gabriel Rossi, which was the name I was given from the library at the Historical Review Board. I slipped a twenty to the maitre d' and was given a seat at Rossi's table, at the edge of the dance floor, near the stage.

The Historical Review Board already had clear evidence of a violation, and had even tracked the likely time portal that was used by Rossi. The only matter that needed to be investigated was whether Rossi was a knowing participant, or merely an identity used by another bad actor. The record at the library had a short bio on Rossi, along with a picture and a description. It seems that Rossi already had earned an extensive record as a con man in the modern era. It only remained to gather some admission on Rossi's part, and I could easily convict him.

There was also an outside chance that Sullivan was involved. Whenever the HRB library printed out an incident report, Sullivan's name always sprang up as being "possibly associated". If the Historical Review Board had a ten most wanted list, Sullivan would have filled all ten.

As one of the top agents at the HRB, I considered Sullivan as a sort of nemesis. I had never personally laid eyes on him, but I felt that I had been very close in bringing Sullivan down on several occasions.

Alba's act ended, and soon she was seated at my table.

"Hello," I said.

"Hello." Alba returned my smile, but it seemed that she was angry at something.

"I loved your act," I said. "You're very talented."

"Thank you," she said. "But don't you think…", Alba halted for a moment and brushed back a tear. "Don't you think that if a person goes through a great deal of trouble, that someone else should have to follow their agreement, even if it isn't written down?"

"Of course," I said. "People should always follow through with their agreements."

"Exactly. I came here, all the way from Portugal, with the understanding that I had a contract. And now, this, this, Rossi…" She broke off again, and started sobbing. I handed her a handkerchief and she wiped her big brown eyes with it.

"Thank you," she said. "I don't mean to be a cry-baby, but it is just so unfair." I liked the way she said "cry-baby".

"Mr. Sullivan promised me that he could extend my visa, and now he has disappeared, and this Rossi is trying to…" She broke off again.

'Sullivan…' I thought.

"So you're about to be deported?" I asked.

Alba nodded. "Do you know how long it takes to go back to Portugal? There's a war going on!" she said.

"What about your boyfriend? Have you discussed it with him?"

"I don't have a boyfriend," she said. "I don't know what you are implying."

She caught me off guard. I suddenly remembered that the Iberian people of that era were fairly conservative. "I only meant to say that if you married a U.S. citizen, you would acquire citizenship and you wouldn't need a visa."

Alba stopped for a moment and blinked her eyes at me. "Is that an offer?" she asked.

I had not intended to suggest that she should enter into a marriage of convenience, but I disliked showing fear when a woman flirted with me. "Try me," I said. In the back of my mind, I knew that I wouldn't have to follow through with anything once Rossi was arrested and the reset happened.

It was just that moment that a tall, fat man in a tuxedo began to seat himself at the table. "Oh, we have another guest," he said. "Is this a friend of yours?"

"This is my fiancé," Alba said.

I held out my hand. "Bob Gordon," I said. I looked into the eyes of the large man and shook his hand. He had big lips and greasy skin, and held his head back proudly, as though he had descended from nobility. It was Gabriel Rossi.

"I didn't know that you were engaged," Rossi said to Alba.

"There's a whole lot that you don't know about me," she said.

"I guess this means you don't need any help getting your visa," Rossi said.

"No, I won't," Alba said flatly.

I guessed that Rossi had been trying to insert some degenerate clause into his agreement with Alba, in light of her desperate need for a work visa.

"I was just telling Alba how much I appreciated your music," I said. "Who writes your music?"

"I do," Rossi said proudly.

"Words and music?"

"That's right," Rossi said. "I write it all myself."

"That's amazing," I said, feigning astonishment. There was a digital camera mounted on my captain's hat that was recording our conversation. 'You're finished,' I thought to myself.

The waiter left a large martini in front of Rossi, and he downed it in one gulp. "Tell me, Bob," he said, holding up his glass for the waiter to refill. "How did you meet Alba?"

"We both know Mr. Sullivan," I said. "In fact, I was hoping to meet with him this evening."

"Oh, the elusive Mr. Sullivan. That makes three of us then," Rossi said, downing his second martini.

"You don't expect him?" I asked, disappointed, but not terribly surprised.

"I haven't seen Sullivan in over a month," Rossi said. "We had some unfinished business. He promised Alba a visa, and you see how that fell through. What's your business with Sullivan?"

I pointed to the sphinx medal on my chest that signified military intelligence. "I'm sorry, that's classified," I said.

Rossi nodded, and I enjoyed watching Rossi's eyes shrink just a little when he perceived that military intelligence was in contact with Sullivan.

Everything about my uniform was perfect, and every credential was perfect. The HRB had no problem fabricating everything to the smallest detail.

"I have to leave now," I said. "Do you mind if I dance with my fiancé?"

I held out my hand to Alba, and we walked out onto the dance floor just as the band began playing 'Our Love is Here to Stay'. It obviously was not one of Rossi's "original" numbers, but the crowd loved it just the same.

I'm a competent dancer, trained in the manners of the time in which I was visiting, and I pulled Alba close as we moved to the music. There's something about music and dancing that makes a person do things they didn't plan, or which don't make much sense. After the reset, Alba wasn't going to remember any of this, but nevertheless, I leaned close into Alba's ear, and I felt her curly hair brush against my lips as I spoke:
"Listen to me. I'm completely serious right now," I said. "I'm going to hold up my end of our agreement. I'm going to be back here in one week, and if you still want to, we can be married. Don't tell anyone, but Rossi's going away tonight." Alba pulled away and looked deeply into my eyes. At that moment I wished that I still had the video camera running so that I could record her smile.

"I'll be here," she said.

I knew she wouldn't, but it felt good to hear her say it anyway. I kissed her hand when the dance ended, and that was all. I walked out of the club, and after a few furtive glances, I casually walked to a phone booth on the sidewalk and used a key to open it.

The phone booth was a time machine, of course. The time machine had made many things possible, but the dangers were just as great. It was the job of the Historical Review Board to be the guardians of time, and to ensure that History remained stable and uncorrupted.

I had been with the HRB for ten years at that point, and before I had been recruited, I had never even heard of the HRB. This was because the very existence of the time machine was classified. I had majored in history and physics, and I had written my thesis on the possibility of creating a time machine. It was all theoretical, of course, but just two weeks after I graduated from university, two HRB agents came to my home and recruited me.

The Historical Review Board was invented in a year that is classified, but it was a few years before I had been born. The HRB library was instituted a short time after the time machine. The main purpose of the HRB was to preserve the continuous thread of time. Even before the time machine was created, it was easy to conceive that even the smallest change in a prior event could have enormous effects on subsequent events. A kingdom could be lost for the want of a horseshoe nail.

As it turns out, in practice, it was found that time was very robust: time seemed to have a preconceived endpoint, and if a minor change was introduced early on, other minor changes would be introduced to make up for that. But even if minor changes were introduced, they could be very profitable to the ones who instituted them. The most obvious example was the theft of intellectual property, such as the copyright that I was protecting back at the jazz club in 1943.

This was the reason for the creation of the HRB library. The library was the repository for all intellectual property, and it also preserved a timeline for the original history that existed before time travel.

The library was a fantastic invention, and it worked something like a burglar alarm. The timeline and all intellectual property had been converted to electronically recorded bits of information, and stored in a library that existed outside of time. The library had ties to copyright and patent libraries, so that if there was ever an attempt to record the same material at an earlier date, the alarm sounded, and the library sent out a notice to agents at the HRB.

Ignatius Sullivan was one of the pioneers of time travel, and the HRB library was primarily his design. So it was a great surprise and disappointment when Sullivan had turned rogue and had fought against the HRB. Although the time machine technology was paid for by the Department of Defense, and every official time machine had a serial number, and a log that was tracked and recorded, Sullivan possessed the knowledge and skill to build his own time machine. It was believed that Sullivan had organized a private army of saboteurs and agents, for it was impossible to otherwise explain all the disruptions reported by the HRB library.

I didn't know where the library existed on the map, and it was said that the library was impossible to reach without a time machine. The idea was that the library, an enormous building of numerous computers and other research materials, existed perpetually in what could physically be described as a state of flux: a moment existing between other moments. All of the government time machines were constructed to reach the library as a sort of home port. Even if you didn't know where you were in time, the library could always be reached in a variety of different navigational modes.

My time machine docked at the library, as it had many times before, and I walked quickly towards the criminal justice section. The case against Rossi had already been laid out beforehand: numerous songs had been registered by Rossi in 1943, some forty to sixty years before they had originally been composed; an unlicensed time machine, believed to be used by Rossi, was recorded as leaving from the time Rossi had gone missing, and arriving in 1943; and now my video evidence proved that Rossi was admitting to the act. The guilty verdict would only a matter of filing the paperwork.

The library was truly gargantuan: endless halls, and hundreds of rooms, each having a special emphasis on some period of history, a type of art, or a branch of literature. A historian could spend a lifetime in the library and never get bored, and possibly never see another soul. I had been to the library many times, but I had rarely seen other users. Most everyone using the library was an agent for the HRB, so there was a very limited clientele spread across a vast area.

Of course, the library had been built on the justification that the invention of the time machine had put the stability of time in jeopardy. Having been born after the time machine, and knowing that history had remained stable my entire life, I felt a certain pride that the HRB had been so successful.

There were always going to be minor corrections, but these were restorations or "resets", which followed the return of some stolen copyright or another article back to its proper date, as I was currently in the process of doing. Minor resets of this sort were hardly experienced by the population. It was believed that those most affected might have a night of strange dreams, but that was all.

I entered the Hall of Copyright and looked around. Despite the grand vision of the HRB Library, most of the cases were filed in the Hall of Copyright, or the Bureau of Patent. Taking an invention to an earlier time was the easiest and most obvious way to turn a quick profit from a time machine. Most people seemed to lack the patience, or intelligence to work out a more complicated scheme that would be more difficult to discover or prosecute.

I loaded the video and other documents into the computer and sent them to the HRB of Justice. The Board of Justice was in another time and location, so the result was nearly instantaneous: A judgment of guilty was printed out with the recommended sentence. As expected, Rossi was going to be permanently banished. The paperwork had a digital stamp from the HRB Library that could not be forged, showing that I now had the power to carry out the sentence. Since agents were vested with so much authority, the guidelines required that agents come into actual possession of the properly stamped paperwork before executing a sentence.

The next stop was the Property Assessor's Office. I needed to decide on a suitable time and place to exile Rossi. The HRB employed agents whose sole purpose was to purchase properties of every sort, in many different eras. Most of the sentences handed down from the Board of Justice were banishment, so it was necessary to have a large selection of properties to which they could be banished. The ultimate destination was left up to the judgment of the prosecuting agent: If the defendant was cooperative, he might get a small home in a medieval town; If the defendant did not cooperate, and if he mistreated beautiful jazz singers, he might get sent to some an isolated shack in Siberia. The important thing is that the defendant should be left in a place where he couldn't cause any more harm. I chose several properties and downloaded the coordinates.

Instead of heading directly back to the time machine, I made one more trip to the Hall of Records. The Hall did not contain the records of every human being who had ever lived, but it held a good percentage. I sat down at one of the corner desks and made a quick search for Alba. She was born in Spain in 1923, but her family moved to Portugal during the Civil War. She went to New York in 1941, and then returned to Portugal. The steamer she was traveling on was torpedoed and sunk in 1943.

Reading about her death filled me with an overwhelming sadness. Until I had met Alba, I hadn't realized how lonely I was. I enjoyed my job, and I felt that my work was meaningful, but I had very little human interaction. Traveling through time was isolating work.

Now I was staring at the screen and realizing that my intervention could have been quite fortuitous for her. If I had married her, she wouldn't have had to leave the country, and she would not have been on that steamer...

It was precisely at that moment that a piece of paper fluttered down, brushing my forehead and landing on the keyboard in front of me. I turned the paper over and read the contents. It contained a screenshot of a New York Times Headline: "KENNEDY IS KILLED BY SNIPER AS HE RIDES IN CAR IN DALLAS; JOHNSON SWORN IN ON PLANE".

I looked above to see where the paper had come from, but I couldn't see anyone. I was alone in the library. There was a digital stamp in the top corner, and the library scanner proved it to be a legitimate item. I tucked the paper into my valise and headed back to the time port.

There was a wide variety of time machine disguises to choose from. This time I picked a time machine that looked like a 1939 Ford Coupe. I set the coordinates, and soon I was on the street outside of the 88 Club in New York, back in 1943. I took sips from a thermos of black coffee while watching employees exit from the club out of the back door. Alba left just after closing time. She caught a cab in the street, and I ducked down low in the seat, so the cab's headlights wouldn't see me as they drove by.

Then I sat back up and waited. About fifteen minutes later, Rossi came out of the club and walked over to a Burgundy Hudson that was parked on the street, just in front of my car.

Rossi unlocked his car door and sat behind the wheel. Just as he was putting the key into the ignition, I opened the passenger door and sat down next to him.

"What are you doing here?" Rossi asked.

I held a gun up so that Rossi could see it, and then handed him a pair of handcuffs. "Put these on," I said. I made sure that the chain of Rossi's cuffs passed through the steering wheel, chaining him to the car. Then I removed the key from the ignition.

"You are under arrest for the violation of code section 506 of the Historic Preservation Act." I showed Rossi a copy of the judgment. "You were tried in absentia, found guilty, and sentenced. Any leniency applied to your case will be dependent upon your cooperation with the investigation."

Rossi's head slumped forward on the steering wheel. "What do you want?" he moaned.

"Tell me when you met Sullivan, and what was the exact time that you took the time machine here."

"What if I don't cooperate?" Rossi asked.

"Asking that question is a sign of non-cooperation. Your punishment just got a little worse. I need to stop you from coming here, obviously. Once I arrest you in the future, all of this goes away. But if I can't arrest you just at the moment before you leave, I might just go back and get you a year before that. What do I care?"

"In my jacket pocket, there's a datebook." Rossi

signaled with his thumbs.

I fetched a datebook out of Rossi's breast pocket and started thumbing through the pages. Rossi's datebook was still from the year in the future he had left.

"You're using the old calendar still?"

"The calendar repeats that year. Why should I buy a new one? Go to May 29," Rossi said.

The page on that date read: "12 NOON. Meet Sullivan. Bring the money and ALL music!!!"

"When did you first meet Sullivan?"

"A week before that."

The calendar verified that fact. "How much did you pay him?" I asked.

"One hundred thousand in gold."

"Did you ever shake hands with Sullivan?"

"What?"

"Cooperate," I said. "Did you ever shake hands?"

Rossi thought for a moment. He shook his head. "No," he said.

I let out a sigh. "Okay, look: I'm going to leave you here with the windows rolled up. When I arrest you in the future, all of this will go away."

"Will I… will I die?" Rossi asked.

"I don't think so ... unless you try to resist arrest." I smiled and patted the gun. "So while you're sitting here, concentrate on not resisting arrest in the future."

I left Rossi there, alone in the car, and Rossi's eyes were closed in deep concentration.

A short time later, I was in front of Rossi's house. I hadn't bothered to change, and I was still wearing the World War II-era Army captain's uniform. I walked to the side gate, and let myself into the backyard. Rossi was standing in the middle of the yard, dressed in Bermuda shorts, a Hawaiian shirt, and sunglasses. A suitcase and several backpacks were at his feet.

"Who are you?" Rossi asked.

I held out the gun towards future Rossi. "Shut up and put these on," I said, handing the cuffs to Rossi again. "You are under arrest for the violation of code section 506 of the Historic Preservation Act," I said, repeating the same arrest procedure I had just done with the same man. It was the law.

The time machine appeared a short time after that, in the form of a tool shed. I motioned for Rossi to be quiet. The door to the shed opened, and out stepped Sullivan, holding a shovel.

"Hello, Mr. Gordon," Sullivan said.

I waved my hand, and it passed through the holograph of Sullivan.

"Maybe someday we will meet in person," Sullivan said.

"Maybe I'll send you on a long vacation," I said. I looked into the shed and saw the device that was projecting Sullivan's holograph.

"Remember to follow through with your agreements," Sullivan said. Then he smiled broadly and said:

"We seek him here, we seek him there,
Those Frenchies seek him everywhere.
Is he in heaven?—Is he in hell?…"

The door to the shed closed suddenly, and suddenly the shed and the hologram both disappeared.

I didn't have the heart to leave Rossi in Siberia. Instead, I put Rossi down on a small island in Ancient Greece. Certainly, it was a lot more rugged than Rossi was used to, but the people were civilized, and he could get by with a little hard work.

Finally, the case was finished, and I was back once more in 1943, behind the wheel of a Ford Coupe. The reset should have happened once Rossi's trip was canceled, but I had to go back and make sure that nothing remained of the historic violations.

My opinion of the HRB had become conflicted since my last visit to the library. I still had that paper with the headline about President Kennedy, and I examined it once more. President Kennedy? Kennedy had lost a very close election to Richard Nixon in 1960, and he went on to become a famous author.

But that paper had the official stamp from the library, which meant that at one time it had been history! Which meant that the official history had been changed by the powers that controlled the library. That meant that the other agents and I were defending a false history. That single paper had made me question the HRB mission. There was corruption at its very heart. I sat there for a while before deciding to keep my last appointment.

Everything looked the same on the outside of the club, and the maitre d' was just as willing to give me a seat at the reserved table, near the stage, for $20.

Alba was still singing onstage, but now the song was from the correct era. When she was finished, Alba came to the table and smiled at me. "Hello," she said.

"Hello," I said. 'She must be wondering who I am right now,' I thought to myself. "Would you like to dance?" I held my hand out to Alba, and the band started playing "Our Love is Here to Stay".

"Doesn't this band know how to play anything

else?" I asked.

"I asked them to play that," Alba said. "Are you still my fiancee?" she asked.

I turned and looked at her. It was impossible that she still knew me. In this timeline, Rossi had never appeared, and I had only come as a consequence… I looked into her dark brown eyes. "How do you remember?"

"It was only a week ago," Alba said. "I'm not senile, you know."

"Listen," I said. "If you still want to go through with this, you have to know some things about me…"

We continued to dance for a long time, and it was clear that Alba was not going to be taking a steamer back to Portugal any time soon.

I turned in my notice to the HRB, and afterward, Alba and I took an early retirement to an undisclosed location. I left a forwarding address on Alba's employment card in the office of Club 88, just in case Sullivan wanted to congratulate us on our marriage.

The End.

9 ASSAYS OF BIAS

Your bait of falsehood takes this carp of truth.
And thus do we of wisdom and of reach,
With windlasses and with assays of bias,
By indirections find directions out.

The sky was an odd shade of orange. It was near sundown, and Thomas was late for a dentist appointment. He hurried through the neighborhood at a fast walk. He looked at the addresses on the houses as he passed, and noticed the numbers for the first time. Thomas had to cover several blocks very quickly to get to his appointment, but it was suddenly important for him to notice that the house numbers went up by eight for each property.

Thomas saw a house that was painted light green, and which had Italian Cypresses that were hedged into interesting shapes. He walked on for half a block and then saw what seemed to be an identical house with the same color and hedges. He wanted to go back and check, but there wasn't time. There was a house number that he was looking for, but he didn't know which house, and he didn't know why it was important.

The dentist's office was at the corner of the next block, at the boulevard, where the suburban housing joined with the commercial district. It had taken him several minutes to walk that far, but the sun hadn't progressed noticeably in that time. The sky was still bright orange when Thomas reached the dentist.

The receptionist was not there to meet him, which he guessed was because he was a little late. Thomas let himself into one of the rooms in the back and sat down in the dentist chair. He had just lain back in the chair when his mother poked her head into the office. She was a stern woman, and she gave Thomas a look that let him know she was upset with him. Then she was gone. Thomas was a little frightened of his mother, and he did not look forward to the lecture he was going to have to hear from her later.

The dentist came in next. Dr. Whitaker. He was thickly built and had hairy forearms.

"Hello, doctor," Thomas said.

"You're late again Thomas," Dr. Whitaker said. He walked over to the sink and began washing his hands very rapidly.

"I'm sorry. I don't know where the time went."

"What were you doing?" the dentist asked.

"I don't know. Playing, I guess."

"Where were you?" Dr. Whitaker began drying his hands on a clean white towel.

"By my house, I think. I'm not really sure. I just noticed that it was getting dark, and I hurried over here so that I wouldn't be late."

"It's very important that you remember things, Thomas. When you have an appointment, you have to be on time, otherwise, you're wasting my time."

"I'm sorry," Thomas said.

The dentist grabbed a probe off of the tray and held up the other hand to Thomas. "Okay, just relax now, and I'll take a look."

Thomas looked at Dr. Whitaker's hairy forearms as he felt the probe searching for cavities.

"Did you notice anything unusual on the way over here?" Dr. Whitaker asked.

"The sky was a weird color of orange," Thomas said.

"Not that," Dr. Whitaker said, sounding a little angry, as though Thomas had given the wrong answer.

"I looked at the house numbers," Thomas added, hoping this was what the Doctor was looking for.

"Yes?"

"I noticed that they went up by eight for each house," he said.

"And what else?"

Thomas couldn't think of anything else. "Just numbers, I guess."

"What did it start with?" Dr. Whitaker asked.

"I don't remember," Thomas said.

"Well, what is your home address?"

Suddenly Thomas realized that he didn't remember his home address. "Gosh, Doc! I can't remember for some reason. I'm sure it's on a card out there in the office."

The dentist could hardly contain his frustration. "You're twelve years old and you don't know your own address?!"

"I know my address. You're just making me nervous," Thomas said.

"Okay, think back: How many houses did you pass?"

Thomas tried to think back. "Uhh…" The probe poked Thomas' gum, and he cried out. "Ouch!"

Dr. Whitaker did not even apologize for poking Thomas, but instead lightly slammed the probe in the tray. "You don't appear to have any cavities, but I'm going to have to use the gas. Do you want to have your mother in here?"

"No, that's okay," Thomas said.

Dr. Whitaker put the mask over Thomas' face. "You've had this before. Just start counting back from twenty."

"Nineteen," Thomas began. "Eighteen, sev…"

The room melted away, and for a moment Thomas perceived that he was enveloped in an orange cloud. He saw his old baseball mitt, perched on top of the dresser in his room. He walked over to the dresser, and upon close inspection, the surface of the wooden dresser appeared to be a computer screen. He touched the dresser with his hand and he saw numbers flashing across the surface of the wood.

Suddenly Thomas found himself in the cabin of a spaceship. He felt a slight, stabbing pain in his side. He looked down and saw that he was wearing a spacesuit, and that he had been wounded by a metal rod that had pierced through his abdomen and out through his back. There were tubes and wires connected to machines that appeared to be feeding him and monitoring his heart rate and blood pressure.

Thomas was frightened by the sudden shift. He saw that his hands and body were larger and man-sized. He looked to his left and saw that there was another astronaut in the cabin. He recognized the other astronaut as his friend … Dr. Whitaker. Of course! How had he forgotten?

He and Whitaker had been on a mission with Olsen. They were doing repairs outside the ship and then … there was an explosion?

"Where's Olsen?" Thomas asked.

Whitaker looked up at Thomas and shook his head. "We lost him. You're lucky to be alive. You keep fading in and out."

Thomas nodded. "I remember everything," he said. He looked at his abdomen, and suddenly a flash of pain shot through where he had been wounded, and Thomas grimaced. Then the pain vanished, just as quickly as it had come.

"Listen, Thomas," Whitaker said, "you have experienced a lot of trauma. You're getting a drip for the pain, and all of your signs are stable. In case your mind gets too stressed, your memory has been wired up to a simulated reality. Whenever your body gets too taxed, the AI kicks in and creates a more relaxed environment."

"Right," Thomas said. "It just seems so real. It's like I was back in my hometown."

Whitaker nodded. "That's good. Now you have to work with me quickly before you fade out again."

"Okay," Thomas said. "What do you need?"

"The explosion destroyed part of the ship's memory. We need to get back to the dock, but we don't have the coordinates. You're the pilot, do you remember that?"

"I think so," Thomas said.

"Now try to remember: Do you know the coordinates of the dock?"

Thomas closed his eyes and tried to think. "I can't remember anything," he said. "I have a general memory of taking off, but nothing stands out in particular."

"Understood. But try to remember any numbers that seem significant. This is vitally important to save the mission."

Thomas thought for a moment. "Uhm, it goes by eights?" he guessed.

Whitaker let out what sounded like a groan of frustration, and Thomas thought he heard a metal object slammed into a tray.

"This obviously isn't working," Whitaker said. "I think you're still under too much stress."

"Yes, it's probably the stress," Thomas agreed.

"I'm going to turn the simulation back on," Whitaker said. Thomas saw Whitaker reach over his head, and he heard him pushing some buttons.

Thomas opened his eyes, and he was back in the dentist's office. He looked down at his abdomen, and saw that he had not been injured, and that his hands were normal-sized.

Thomas looked around the office. "Doc?"

Doctor Whitaker came into the office. "You were asleep for a long time," he said.

"Yeah? I had the weirdest dream," Thomas said.

"The gas will do that," Dr. Whitaker said. "Don't worry about it. Everything is fine. I won't have to see you for another six months."

"Great," Thomas said, getting up out of the chair.

"Your mother already left. She said she would see you at home." Dr. Whitaker opened to door for Thomas.

"Okay. I guess I'll see you in about six months."

Thomas walked past the receptionist's desk, let himself out of the front door, and started down the sidewalk. It was pitch dark outside, but Thomas couldn't make out any stars. He assumed that there was a thick cloud cover.

He was passing by a large bush when he heard a voice call out.

"Hey, kid," the voice said.

Thomas turned to the bush. "Who is that?"

"I'll come out, but you have to keep it down. Don't talk too loudly. Just nod your head, okay?"

Thomas nodded his head.

A man came out of the bushes. He was an older man, with grey hair and spectacles. The man was smiling and had bright blue eyes.

"Hello Thomas," the old man said.

Thomas started to say 'hello', but the man's eyes darted up, as if to warn him. Thomas caught himself, and nodded hello, and smiled.

"Everything seems a little strange lately, doesn't it?" the man said.

Thomas nodded.

"Follow me." The man gestured, and they started walking back towards the dentist's office.

There was a large window to the office, and the man walked right up to the window and peeked in. He motioned for Thomas to look in the window.

Thomas saw that the light was on inside the office, but it wasn't the same office that he had just left. Inside, a man lay on a sort of dentist chair, and there were many wires and tubes inserted into his head, arms, and abdomen. The tubes and wires ran to several different machines. There were three other men in the room: one of them was monitoring the equipment, and the other two were having a conversation. One of the men was Dr. Whitaker. He appeared to be very upset at something.

"Do you see what's going on?" the old man asked.

Thomas nodded, but he didn't understand.

"Do you know what they're doing?"

Thomas shook his head.

"The man on the chair is being interrogated. They are using drugs and artificial simulations."

Thomas was shocked. Dr. Whitaker was doing interrogations in his office?

The old man put his hand on Thomas' shoulder. "There's nothing we can do. We can't call the police. They won't come."

Thomas took a deep breath and nodded his head.

The old man led Thomas by the sleeve. "We've seen enough."

The two walked back towards the bush where Thomas and the old man had originally met. The old man continued, "On the bright side, they aren't getting anywhere with their interrogation. The man in the chair is protected, you see. Before he was captured, he created a simulation of his own. It allows a person to avoid any sort of compelled interrogation. The person being interrogated will be impervious to pain or any other torture device.

"Of course they won't give up. They're trying to get information by dredging up associated memories and then somehow piecing them together. But it won't work."

Thomas felt reassured, although he had no idea who the man was.

"It won't last much longer," the old man said. "Sooner or later, the man's body will give out."

It made Thomas sad to hear this, and the old man put a gentle hand on his shoulder.

"But even if he dies, he will still have won. So don't be too sad. He's a very brave man."

A tear escaped from Thomas' eye, even though he

did not know the man.

"I had to let you see that, Thomas. I thought you should understand."

The two of them stood together silently for a moment. Then the man spoke up. "You live with your mother, right?"

Thomas nodded his head.

"And your father died when you were very young."

Thomas nodded, sadly.

"Well, I'm sure your father would be very proud of you, Thomas. You're a very good boy. Now listen: don't pay any attention to what that dentist says about you remembering anything. Just enjoy your life. Go and explore the world. Find new things. You won't be a boy forever."

Thomas nodded and waved goodbye to the man. It made him feel good to know that his dad would have been proud of him. He started to walk home.

Soon it was evening, and the sky was bright orange. Thomas was late for a doctor's appointment.

The End.

STRANGE CAPERS

10 TO FIND A BAREFOOT BROTHER

Going to find a barefoot brother out,
One of our order, to associate me,
Here in this city visiting the sick,
And finding him, the searchers of the town,
Suspecting that we both were in a house
Where the infectious pestilence did reign,
Sealed up the doors and would not let us forth.
So that my speed to Mantua there was stayed.

The year was 1880, and I was working on a freighter taking our first load of sugar from Hawaii to San Francisco. Hawaii was known then as the 'Sandwich Islands', ruled by King Kalākaua. Many of the plantations on the islands were run by wealthy industrialists, who had a strong influence over the government.

We had docked in Honolulu, and being a sailor, I found my way to the nearest tavern. I had heard other sailors speak lovingly of the local rum drinks that were mixed with tropical juices, and I was eager to try some of these on for size.

I was waiting to order one of these drinks, and I

heard a man ordering drinks in an accent that sounded like it came from my native state of Tennessee. The man speaking looked to be in his forties and was not dressed like a merchant sailor, but instead, he wore the clothes of a frontiersman. He had a broad-brimmed hat, a handkerchief tied around his neck, a white shirt underneath a floral vest, and boots that went all the way up to his knees. The one concession he had made to the humid climate was to take off his fringed deerskin jacket.

My fellow Tennesseean had staked off a dark corner table all to himself, and no one else seemed to desire, or even dare to invite themselves to join him. Perhaps this was due to the enormous rifle that leaned against the wall at his elbow. But I went ahead and sat down, introducing myself as a native of Memphis.

Thankfully his exterior was more cruel than his spirit, and he held out his hand and welcomed me. His name was Jack Hinton, he hailed from Johnsonville, Tennessee. Jack was drinking his rum straight, but it didn't seem to lighten his spirits much. The corners of his mouth were turned down, and I asked him what the matter was.

"It was a tragic day," he said. "I'm still quite shaken up about it, and I appreciate your company."

And then he began to tell me his story.

I was twenty years old when they fired on Fort Sumpter. My father owned a large plantation near Johnsonville, and I was one of ten children. We had pretty much everything we needed back then, and I had a very happy childhood.

My father refused to support the Confederacy and had stood strongly for the Union. Our state, as you know, was heavily divided: supplying most of the soldiers for the Confederacy, and the most for the Union of any southern state. In fact, I had brothers fighting on both sides in the war of Northern aggression.

It was sometime after Grant was made head of the Union forces, that they came to our neck of the woods, and my father invited General Grant to stay at our plantation as a guest. My father had freed all his slaves, but they had chosen to stay on and work as free men. Grant liked our plantation so much that he set up his center of operations there.

In Tennessee back then, some fought on the rebel side in open combat, but some rebs would hide in the bushes, and fire on Union troops while they were marching, or during a retreat. The Yankees called these types "bushwhackers", and they warned that this type of warfare would be severely punished.

So it was one day that my two younger brothers went out hunting in the woods near our plantation. My brothers were only 12 and 14, barefoot, and armed with small-bore squirrel rifles, but I reckon that didn't make any difference to the Yankee lieutenant who was paid a bounty to capture bushwhackers. The Yankees executed my brothers by firing squad and cut their heads off. Then they stuck their heads on pikes and hung them up in front of our plantation.

Up until that day, I was indifferent to the outcome of the war. Like my father, I had believed in the Union, and I did not want to fight my countrymen. But the merciless slaughter of my little brothers seemed even more unjust because we had treated the Northern Army as honored guests.

My father's library had translations of some of the ancient works, and I remembered that line from Euripides about the Trojan war: Menelaus says that he didn't come to Troy so much to get his wife back, but to punish Paris, the man who ate with him and then stole Helen from his house: "A traitor to my hospitality."

From then on I was a diehard enemy of the North. They killed my brothers for being bushwhackers, so I decided to show them what a real bushwhacker could do. I had a gun made, with a 41-inch barrel, that could shoot accurately over half a mile, and I went on the hunt for union soldiers.

The first one was the lieutenant that ordered the killing of my brothers. Then I found the others involved and shot them as well. It wasn't long after that the Union Army discovered who was sniping after them, and they put a bounty on my head.

A unit was assigned to my capture, but I had grown up in those woods, and they were all foreign invaders. Evading them in my own backyard was child's play. I would leave a false trail into a clearing, and then seek the high ground, and pick off one or two of them when they came into the open. It was almost too easy for me.

Once, I was forced to flee into a mountain cave near to where the rivers forked, by Johnsonville. The waters slowed down there, and the boats always came almost to a standstill, right in my line of fire. From up in my perch, I could make out the officer on deck through my rifle sites, and after the officer went down, the boat would go into a full panic.

Every time I shot an officer, I put a notch in my rifle. There's thirty-three of them there, and I reckon there are another one hundred enlisted men I shot before the war ended.

After the war, I couldn't stay in Tennessee: The Union troops had burnt our plantation down, and I was too well known. I couldn't risk reprisal from my former enemies, so I went out West.

In California, there were a lot of opportunities, but the easiest money was in chasing down outlaws. Bandits and thieves would commit atrocities, and then flee out West, so large bounties would be posted for their capture or death. 'Dead or Alive' posters promised more for a single bounty than a man could earn in several years.

I found that I was well suited to this work. All I had to do was find the man's stomping grounds, and get a positive identification from a couple of the locals. I took pains to make sure that my investigations were unobserved so that no one would warn the man I was chasing. But I noticed that most criminals are notorious because they enjoyed being notorious. Such men are easy to find.

I never tried to capture anyone alive, but I chose instead to snipe at them when they went out alone. No one ever saw it coming, and I was usually working from a thousand feet away. I didn't feel guilty about it because they only issued a 'dead or alive' reward for someone if he was a known murderer.

I had my rifle and a pack mule. After killing an outlaw, I would tie him to the back of my mule and go to collect my money. The sheriff in the nearest town could make the identification and authorize the reward.

After ten years of this, I already had a sizable nest egg. I also made quite a reputation among the judges and lawmen, but I had no intention of becoming notorious. If I became generally recognizable, that would only make my work more difficult.

It was at this point that I was contacted by an emissary from the Sandwich Islands, who had been sent by several of the local large growers. It seems I had been recommended to them by a judge in San Francisco that had wired a few bounties to me.

The emissary told me that they were having trouble with a leper who had escaped. He had been some sort of a local chieftain, or warrior, that had somehow contracted the leprosy. You see, back when the islands had been discovered, the population numbered in the hundreds of thousands. But after exposure to Western diseases, the indigenous population experienced a rapid decline. Smallpox had taken many, and a massive inoculation program was instigated to contain it.

I don't know if you've ever studied vaccines, but the principle is very simple: You expose people to a disease so that they can acquire some immunity. In the case of smallpox, the practice is to expose people to a harmless disease called "cowpox". It turns out that someone who has been exposed to cowpox will be immune to smallpox, which, as you know can be quite deadly.

The method most commonly employed for vaccinations is called "arm-to-arm". That's where the doctor makes a small incision in a person's arm, and then takes the lymph out of the lesions from someone with smallpox, and inserts them into the incision. After that person is inoculated, a doctor can use those lesions and insert that lymph into more people. I know it sounds crazy, but that's what they do.

During the war, we were short of doctors, and when there was a smallpox epidemic, some of the fellows on the front lines would resort to self-inoculation. But the problem often arose where you couldn't tell a cowpox lesion from a syphilis lesion. Some poor fellow would be thinking that he was saving himself from smallpox, and would be getting a venereal disease.

That's why doctors prefer to culture the vaccine in

the arms of children. That way, they can avoid passing on adult diseases. But a similar problem could result in the spread of other, undetected diseases, like leprosy. Now I don't know if that was the cause of leprosy in the Sandwich Islands, but leprosy was unknown in the islands before their interaction with the West, and suddenly they had so many lepers that they needed to make a colony on one of their islands.

King Kamehameha V declared that a leper colony should be established on the island of Moloka'i. On the north side of that island, was a wide, flat peninsula that was surrounded on three sides by the sea, and to the south was a virtual wall created by sea cliffs that rose 1700 feet in the air. The geographical features formed a natural prison.

The emissary told me that this local chieftain had been placed in the leper colony, but had somehow escaped. He had climbed up the cliff walls, and hidden himself in the jungles of Moloka'i. Every so often he would raid supplies from the nearby towns, and grab chickens or a goat, and the legend about him grew. The local people lived in fear of the leper, and tales about him spread to the other islands.

The plantation owners on Moloka'i appealed to the King, and a hunting party was arranged. Their thinking was that the colony was created to protect people from an incurable disease, and if a leper escaped from the colony then the penalty should be death.

A party of five went out to find the leper, but they never came back. The townspeople waited, but there was no sign. They couldn't understand it. Five men with guns and supplies couldn't capture a single man with no gun?

Another hunting party went out in search of the

first, and they were quite surprised to find that all of the men had been killed on the trail. They had all perished from deep stab wounds to the neck. It appeared as though the chieftain had armed himself with a long knife.

It was difficult to gather another hunting party to go after this leper chieftain. Hunters from the other islands were sought, and finally, another six men went into the jungle in pursuit. This time, one of the porters returned the next day, and that was all. He told of an attack in the middle of the night. The leper attacked them suddenly and brutally. The porter ran for his life and did not stop until he reached the town.

After that, it was impossible to raise another hunting party. The leprous chieftain had now reached the status of a legend. The locals invested him with magical powers and super strength. They believed that the chieftain had been given these powers to strike vengeance upon the Western society that had ravaged the Hawaiian people with disease. The local people talked about the deep stab wounds, and they wondered if these were not symbolic of the vaccinations that had come at the same time as the smallpox and the leprosy.

The legend grew in all of the islands, and everyone came to know about the vengeful specter of the leprous chieftain. The common people started to wonder if they too, ought to resist the strange new ways of Western civilization. This made the plantation owners deeply concerned: It might start as a defiant look, but that would soon grow into a failure to perform duties. After that, there would be insubordination and stubborn refusals.

The plantation owners decided to seek help from outside of the islands. They sent an emissary to San Francisco to recruit an expert at hunting people, and that's where I came in. All of the judges and lawmen said that I was the best.

After hearing the emissary's story, I was reluctant to take the job. I wasn't afraid, but I knew that my strength lay in being able to shoot my enemy from a half-mile away. I could engage an enemy from a distance with very little risk, but if I was hunting this fellow in the jungle, my strength was taken away. I knew that I was a decent tracker, but after I caught up to him, what would I do? In the jungle, I would be facing the enemy at arm's length, and we would be fighting on his ground. So my first thought was to refuse. But then the emissary told me the offer: They would pay me $20,000 in gold, with half up front. If I was successful, hunting the leper would be the last job I would ever need to take.

After seeing the money wired to my account in a Frisco bank, I purchased pistols and ammunition, and enough supplies for three men to live out in the wilderness for two weeks. I also had purchased a pair of foxhounds, which I had found to be very helpful hunting game in the woods in Tennessee. I decided to take my long gun, even though I didn't think it would be of much use, and I caught the next steamer to the Sandwich Islands.

I landed at the port here in Honolulu and sought out some competent men for my hunting party. I met two Filipino brothers, Ephraim and Ernesto, in a bar, and they seemed eager enough to go on the adventure. They weren't large men, but they seemed brave enough, and they were new to the islands, and so they hadn't heard tell of the leper chieftain.

We took a boat out to the island of Moloka'i and docked at Kaunakakai, where we met with the representatives of the growers, and they showed me a tintype photo of the chieftain. The next morning, we started off early into the jungle. A campfire had been spotted due north just the day before, and we used that as our general heading.

Not long after we left the village, we were enveloped by a thick forest of knotted tree trunks, that appeared to be ancient vines which had reached the top of the forest canopy, and had grown fat with age. These trunks were, in turn, covered in a tangle of other vines, and the overall effect was to leave the forest in a perpetual shadow. The floor of the jungle forest was carpeted with ferns and large stones that were covered in moss. Some meandering trails appeared to be headed in the general direction that we wanted to go, but these would often end in a nearly impassable forest that we had to hack our way through with machetes. My companions, Ephraim and Ernesto, were used to this sort of travel, since their own native country was similarly landscaped.

Before nightfall, we found the campsite from where the smoke had been emanating. It was now abandoned, of course. From what we had seen thus far, it seemed an ideal spot to set up a camp, and the fireplace still had some embers that could be stoked back to life.

We ate a meal from the provisions that we had brought and then settled in. Ernesto took the first watch. The night air was warm enough, and I was tired from the day's journey, so it wasn't long before I was asleep.

The attack came silently and without warning. I awoke to the sound of a dull thud, which I later reckoned to be a club hitting the head of one of my foxhounds. I rose quickly, but the forest was black as pitch, and there was no light for me to see our assailant.

"Ernesto! Ephraim!" I called out to my companions, but it was already too late. Neither one responded, and I could only hear the faint groaning of a man who had been fatally wounded.

The chieftain had the advantage of knowing our positions, and eyes that had already adjusted to the dark. I had my long gun in my hand, and I swung it around blindly. I felt it hit someone behind me, to my left. I turned to look, but I couldn't see anything.

I knew that I was a goner if I stayed, so I fled into the darkness. My feet were finding trails through pure happenstance, but more than once my head collided with a low-hanging trunk.

I must have given my assailant a good blow on the head because I got a pretty good lead out before he gave pursuit. I stopped to catch my breath, and I could hear a rustle in the jungle behind me. The chieftain was going to try to kill all of us.

I continued onward, desperately finding a way through that black jungle. I wasn't headed in any particular direction, but I hoped that if I could stay ahead until daybreak, I would be safe. When I stopped for a rest, I would listen, and it seemed as though the rustling behind me was growing closer. I didn't know what time it was, but I started to believe that my chances of staying alive until daybreak were not very good.

And then, just as quickly as my fortunes had faded, they were once again revived. I don't know if you're familiar with foxhounds, but you can hear one of them baying in the forest from miles off. I reckon that the chieftain only stunned one of my hounds, because I heard him baying, far back behind me at the campsite.

"Come on, boy!" I yelled. "Come and get him!"

The hound continued with his noise, and I started away again with a renewed vigor. I knew that the hound would be upon my pursuer before long. The baying that had been so comforting to me would have sent fear into the heart of the leper chieftain. He must have known that he would soon be feeling the angry, gnashing teeth of the dog he had just failed to kill.

The dog caught up to the trail in about half that time it took me, and I soon heard the barking and yelping sounds that a foxhound makes when he is harassing his prey. The man I bought the hounds from had told me he bred them for hunting bear, so I knew that the hound would be pretty fearless.

I listened for a spell while I caught my breath, and I heard the chieftain starting off in another direction. He was no longer chasing me, but now he was trying to get away from the hound.

I turned back, and all at once, I was in the familiar position of a hunter following the baying of the hound as he gave chase to the prey. I kept up as best I could, shouting encouragement to the foxhound. The chieftain still had enough fight left in him, and I must have spent another hour following him and the dog along another rambling path through the forest.

Finally, the sun began poking its way through the canopy, and even though it was still mostly shadow, my eyes could make out my surroundings much more clearly. The terrain had banked up slightly, and I wondered if the chieftain was heading back over the mountains to the leper colony.

Following the hound's barking, I climbed to the top of a small ridge, and there he was, scratching and barking at the base of a tree. I looked up, and at last, I beheld the chieftain. There was enough sun at this point that I could make out his features, and identify him from the tintype photograph I had been shown. In the tintype, the chieftain had been wearing Western-style clothing, but now, up in the tree above my baying hound, I saw that he wore the traditional loincloth, and was naked from the waist up. A club hung from a belt at his waist, and in one of his hands was a long dagger made of fishbone. His left shoulder and bicep were heavily tattooed, and a silver crucifix hung from around his neck.

I stood at the foot of the tree with my loaded rifle and tried to consider my options at that point. There was no way that I could safely transport the chieftain back, but I had no desire to kill him either. Perhaps it would have been an easier decision if he had only been a savage, but the cross around his neck told me that he was a baptized Christian. And yet, I had killed over a hundred Northerners in the war, and probably most, if not all of them were Christians.

Perhaps it was because it didn't seem sporting, to shoot a man who has been treed like a raccoon, or a wild bear. And yet I had killed quite a few wanted outlaws without any sporting chance. Of course, they had all been robbers and murderers.

I looked up at him, and he looked down at me, and I just couldn't bring myself to do it. I lowered the barrel of the gun and called off the dog. "Come on, boy," I said. And the dog turned to follow me.

I guess the chieftain didn't understand that I was letting him off the hook. I had just taken a few steps away when I heard him bounding down and sprinting towards me. The dog started barking again, and I barely got a shot off in time.

The chieftain fell dead in front of me, and the dog started to go after him. I called off the dog because I didn't know if dogs could spread the leprosy or not. I knelt, beside the chieftain, and examined him. He had stopped breathing, but the fingers of his hand were still tightly wrapped around his knife.

His fingers! I looked closely at his hand and saw that he still had all the fingers on his right hand. Then I examined his left hand, and it, too, was completely intact. His face was the same as the face in the tintype. He didn't have any marks or scars from leprosy anywhere on his body. There was only the one large bullet hole that I had just made through his chest.

It was impossible. If he had been a leper for that long, he would have already experienced substantial decay. This man had either been miraculously cured or misdiagnosed. Either way, I was clearly in the wrong for hunting him down.

Jack Hinton's story broke off at that moment when a foxhound trotted into the bar and sat at his feet. "Where have you been?" Hinton asked the dog, who silently looked up at him, and then lay his chin on the man's boots.

Hinton pulled a silver crucifix out of his pocket and stared at it. "I just can't square it with myself," he said. "I've killed a lot of men, but I was always justified. Killing this man, I was no better than those Yankees who shot my brother. I'm no longer justified," he said.

The End.

11 HIS BONES ARE CORAL MADE

Full fathom five thy father lies;
Of his bones are coral made;
Those are pearls that were his eyes;
Nothing of him that doth fade,
But doth suffer a sea-change
Into something rich and strange.

After watching Mr. Doucette remove the faceplate, exposing the circuit board underneath, Thomas could no longer doubt that he was talking to a robot.

"Could you put it back on, now?" Thomas asked.

"Of course."

Doucette expertly snapped the faceplate back into place, and Thomas closely examined the connection. It was perfectly flush, and it was nearly impossible to discern any seam.

"It's an excellent fit, no?" Doucette said, noticing Thomas's curiosity.

Thomas nodded and drew back. He had only just met Mr. Doucette and did not want to seem too familiar, even if Mr. Doucette was not a person.

Thomas had been contacted by Doucette only the day before and had agreed to meet him in the solitary bungalow, just off the highway, not far from where Thomas had grown up. Doucette was using the bungalow using as an office.

"So my father built you for me before he died?" Thomas asked.

"That's correct."

Thomas was silent for a moment, and then spoke a little more loudly than he had intended.

"My father died when I was five years old, and you're just telling me this now? I'll be turning 30 this year."

"Yes," the robot said.

Thomas felt a tear on his eye and wiped it away angrily. He didn't know why he felt so suddenly emotional. He was normally very reserved.

"That's all? Yes? You could at least apologize," Thomas said.

"I'm sorry," the robot said.

Thomas looked at the ground and shook his head. An apology from a robot was even less satisfying when it sounded totally insincere.

Just before meeting Mr. Doucette, Thomas had been very satisfied with his life. He had a good family life, several healthy children, and a very successful electronics business. Now, suddenly Thomas felt as though he had been deprived of something that, moments before, he hadn't even known he was entitled to.

"I mean, what good is having a robot helper that doesn't help you?" Thomas wondered aloud.

"I see," Mr. Doucette said, nodding. Doucette's mannerisms and tone were reassuring, even though

Thomas knew them to be only imitations of human behavior.

"My programming was need-based. Your father felt that if you knew of my presence, you might become too dependent. I was to provide support only when I perceived some inadequacy, and I never felt that I was needed."

"So you just monitored my life?"

"That's right," Doucette said. "I've always kept an eye on your development. You've done very well for yourself."

Inside, Thomas was surprised by the emotions he felt. Somewhere inside of him was a young boy, robbed of the chance to show off his omnipotent robot buddy to all of his classmates. He tried to justify his feelings of deprivation by thinking of instances where the robot should have helped him more.

"You could have tutored me in school," Thomas said.

"You excelled in school," the robot replied. "You graduated from university with honors."

"You could have made it easier," Thomas said.

"Thomas, I think we both know the value of hard work. You put in the sweat, and you benefited a great deal from that."

"How about sports? You could have coached me."

"You did very well in sports, Thomas. I followed your progress in the newspapers. You were all-city in high school, and you were the starting running back at your university."

"But if you coached me, maybe I could have played pro ball."

"Don't be silly, Thomas," the robot said.

Thomas thought for a moment. "You could have

helped me with my business," he said.

"How?" the robot asked. "You've been very successful in business. You're only thirty years old and you've got a thriving business. That was all due to your own initiative."

Thomas couldn't argue the point. He had to admit that his life was pretty good, just as had always felt. He hadn't needed the robot's help. He was doing all right by himself.

"It just seems wasteful, that's all," Thomas said. "My father spent a lot of time making you for me, and you didn't do anything."

"It's the thought that counts," Mr. Doucette said. "I also spent some of my time helping those less fortunate than you."

Thomas felt a jealous rage boiling up in him, but he fought it down, and merely clenched his fists instead.

"What do you do all day? Is this where you live?"

The robot nodded. "I don't need much. I run on electricity, and I plug myself in right over there," he said, gesturing to a wall outlet. "There's a plug at my ankle."

Mr. Doucette, the robot, gestured towards a metal rack with several computers. "Over there is the diagnostic equipment."

He opened a cabinet. "And this is where I keep the tools that I use for minor repairs."

"You do the repairs on yourself?" Thomas asked.

"That's right," Mr. Doucette said. "Your father made me entirely self-sufficient."

"So now what?" Thomas asked. "What is the purpose of disclosing all of this to me now?"

"Yes, there is a point," Mr. Doucette agreed. "I have come to the end of my usefulness. I was only designed to last for twenty-five years, which are up today."

Doucette crossed the room and opened a small file cabinet. He quickly retrieved a single page of slightly yellowed paper and handed it to Thomas.

Thomas read the short paragraph that was typewritten there:

"Dear Thomas,
If you are reading this letter, this means that Mr.

I do not desire that my robot design be used for any nefarious purposes, and so I wish that he be destroyed.

I hope that you can put aside your personal feelings for your robot guardian, and I request that you act diligently to assist Mr. Doucette in carrying out my final wishes.

Love,
Dad"

The letter was signed in the scrawl Thomas recognized as his father's. Thomas had always dearly loved his father, and there was no question that he would do as his father had requested, without any regard for how much the robot might be worth. The part in the letter about overcoming his sentiments for the robot was slightly humorous to Thomas, given the barely suppressed hostility that he currently felt towards Mr. Doucette. He would almost gladly destroy the robot.

"What do you need me to do?" Thomas asked as he handed the letter back to Doucette.

"It will all be very easy for you, given your experience with electronic equipment," the robot said. "I have already arranged all the tools for you right here," he said, opening a small toolbox. "I can talk you through it up until you need to disassemble my voice box and main circuit board. We'll just save that until last."

"That's it?" Thomas asked.

"As you can see, there are three bins: The body will be divided into toxic and recyclable parts. And the last bin is for parts that will need to burn for security purposes. You can do that at your house. You brought your truck, I assume."

"That's right," Thomas said.

"Good. Then you take all the boxes with you. There's just the file cabinet and tools, and a few odds and ends," Mr. Doucette said. "There's a car in the garage. That and the bungalow go back to the estate, so it will belong to your mother. Shall we begin?"

Thomas was a little surprised at the robot's eagerness to meet his oblivion. "Aren't you afraid?" Thomas asked.

Mr. Doucette smiled. "Robots do not feel fear. If I were to describe anything I feel as akin to emotion, it would be happiness at doing exactly what my programming requires. Doing your father's wishes are what makes me happy, and now that means instructing you on how to disassemble my body. Are you ready?"

Thomas nodded. "I guess so," he said.

"Okay," the robot said. "Let's start with my feet…"

When the plastic skin was pulled back from over the metal substructure, Mr. Doucette's body looked much less like that of a human, and thus, much easier to cut into pieces.

Doucette gave instructions on how to undo small springs and other intricate parts that might prove difficult without any aid. Thomas was familiar with all of the tools and techniques, and he had enjoyed doing this sort of work since he was a boy. His mother had often told Thomas about his father's expert skills as a welder and machinist. She was also very proud that Thomas' father, himself only a self-taught electrical engineer, possessed skills that led many factory owners to employ him as a consultant on difficult matters.

It had always been Thomas's goal to become an expert like his father. Thomas studied electrical engineering in college, but he knew how to weld metal and assemble circuit boards from his youth. There was an old retired man in his neighborhood who had taught Thomas how to use tools, and how to weld, and how to put engines together.

Thomas thought about those old times working on cars as he disconnected a circuit board from the robot's midsection, and then disassembled the circuit board. Doucette gave specific instructions on which parts he considered trade secrets, and what exactly needed to be destroyed before placing the parts into the bins.

"Excellent work," Mr. Doucette said, after several hours.

Thomas was almost finished. "The next piece is my voice box, and then you need to dismantle the main motherboard. I won't be able to direct you after this, but you seem to have the situation well in hand."

Thomas moved the screwdriver up towards the voice box, and he heard Mr. Doucette say, "There's just one more item I wanted to play for you before we continue. Just a moment."

There was a slight pause, and then, from out of the voice box came the recording of a different voice. Thomas recognized it as that of his father: "This is my last communication to you, son. I'm very sorry that I couldn't be there with you today. This robot was the next best thing I could do. I put all my love for you and your mother into making this. I hope he served you well. Goodbye."

Thomas was frozen for a moment. His eyes were closed. He hesitated.

"You may continue, Thomas," the robot said.

Thomas loaded all of the boxes and tools into the back of his truck and drove home. He knew it was best not to inform his mother about the robot. If she had known, she never would have let him destroy it, even though it was his father's last wish. Thomas's mother adored his father, and she couldn't bear to part with anything he made.

He drove the ten-minute trip in silence, thinking about the stories his mother had told him about his father. She often said that his father was the most original man she had ever known. Whenever he worked on a project, he would do it in his own, original way. And he always wanted everything done right. He was a hard worker, she said, but he didn't care about becoming rich. She said that his father felt that money caused people to cut corners, and to do wrong things. In the end, this often caused people to make things that didn't work right, or that broke down on purpose.

Thomas remembered speaking to his father on a few occasions when he was very young, but over time, most of his actual memories had blended with the old home videos he had watched, and with the stories that his mother had told him. He remembered being told that his father was sick, but a five-year-old cannot understand the implications of cancer, and he had no idea that his father would be dead a year later. During that time, his father had built the robot and had made sure that there was enough money for his family to get by. They weren't poor, but they weren't rich by any means. They had enough, and they got by alright.

The day after deconstructing the robot, Thomas was going through the boxes in his garage and trying to determine which of the papers needed to be burned. Mr. Doucette was the CEO of the Doucette Corporation, which owned all of the property and accounts. The papers transferring Doucette's property had already been faxed to the attorney who handled the estate, so there was no reason to hang on to the legal fiction that was Mr. Doucette. All of those papers went into the metal can for burning.

There was one box that he hadn't noticed the night before: it was sealed with packing tape, and "Do Not Open!" was written on the side. Thomas didn't consider it a breach of his agreement to open the box, and besides, he didn't know if it was proper, or even safe to burn the contents of the box.

He carefully used a boxcutter to slice through the tape, and found that the box contained several spare masks that he assumed were used by Mr. Doucette. Taking the box over to his workbench, he laid the masks out, side by side, and they gave the impression of an acting troupe.

The faces had only holes where the eyes of the robot looked through, and so they looked lifeless and strange to Thomas. But one mask had a chin with a large wart, that reminded him of the retired machinist who had taught Thomas how to weld. Thomas tried to remember the old man's name. Ray?

There were several old several photo albums that Thomas kept in his living room, and he found a candid photo that his mother had snapped of Thomas and Ray working together in the garage. He held up the robot mask to the old photo and saw that they were identical.

Going back to his ensemble of masks, Thomas examined them more closely and tried to see if there were any other matches with people from his past. He quickly discerned that one of the masks was the face of Mr. Fitzsimmons, who his favorite teacher in junior high school, and who had taught him calculus.

Another mask was the same as the face of Coach Conrad, the assistant football coach. Thomas remembered Coach Conrad had pushed him very hard, and at the time he felt that the coach had been harder on him than all the other players: He made Thomas run more laps, and Thomas had to do more drills than anyone else. Looking back, Thomas remembered it was during that year that he had worked with Coach Conrad that Thomas had made the starting team, and was voted all-city.

Thomas found that one of the masks was the same as the face of the graduate student Thomas had met in university. Thomas forgot how they came to know each other, but they would often meet for lunch in the cafeteria, and the graduate student taught Thomas how to study more effectively, how to organize his time, and how to plan large projects.

One mask was the perfect match for Mr. Smith, one of his scouting leaders. Mr. Smith taught Thomas how to fish and how to set up camp. They had even gone deer hunting together on several occasions.

After emptying the box of all the masks, Thomas could not escape the fact that the robot had indeed lied: all of the masks matched up with men who had mentored Thomas throughout his life. His father's gift to him had indeed been useful. There was no way he could have brought himself to destroy Mr. Doucette if he had known the truth. As it was, he couldn't bear to part with any of the masks either.

Thomas finished filling the metal can with papers that needed to be destroyed, including the driver's license issued to Mr. Doucette, and burned them in his backyard. Afterward, Thomas and his mother bought some flowers and visited his father's grave.

The files also contained notebooks and plans on how to build a robot, and these Thomas placed in his safe. Thomas thought that he might try his hand at building a robot of his own someday.

The End.

ABOUT THE AUTHOR

Henry Garon is an attorney living in San Diego. He likes to barbecue and swim.

Made in the USA
Columbia, SC
20 June 2021